The Day after Yesterday

Douglas Fox
The Day After Yesterday

Cover photo: Fredrik Öhlander unsplash
Spine and title page photo: Bru-nO pixabay (modified)

ISBN: 978-1-7923-9783-7
Library of Congress Control Number: 2022917022
BISAC: FIC028000, FIC028080, FIC009030, FIC022060

This is a work of fiction. Names, characters, places, and incidents either are the products of the author's imagination or are used fictitiously. Any resemblance to actual persons, living or dead, businesses, companies, events, or locales is entirely coincidental.

CONTENTS

Chapter One
Dilemma

Time travel is such a bitch.

Going forward in time is easy enough, and it usually happens a lot faster than we'd like. Skipping time and vaulting forward is no trick. Jumping backward doesn't seem like it should be any big deal, either. After all, the laws of physics are supposed to be timesymmetrical.

It occurred to Eryk Samicki, PhD, that the problem with time travel was just the nuisance of overcoming entropy, the law that says that, on average, disorder has to increase with time. Perhaps adjusting entropy while one travelled back in time might be the key.

Entropy might not be a problem jumping forward. But it's the trip back in time, revisiting the past, or the return trip back from the future that will kill you. In fact, it can kill a lot of people.

The greatest danger arises from traveling to the past while knowing what the future will bring; the time traveler has the power to change history, to annihilate the future, everyone's future. They say knowledge is power but knowledge of the future is death. Yours and mine.

Not that it's a huge technical puzzle anymore. It takes enormous amounts of energy concentrated in a small segment of space-time, but the National Intelligence Administration has solved the problem. People wonder about the mysterious blackouts that occasionally plague the eastern half of the country, but that's just a cost of the experiments that had to be carried out.

Dr. Samicki thought all of this over. If you go back to the past, you don't dare act on your knowledge, in fact, you dare not disturb anything at all in the slightest way. If you don't fit in perfectly, if you let one misconceived remark slip out, if you carry out a single action on the basis of future knowledge, you change that future and there is no way to take it back. Make the slightest alteration in the course of events and the future will be different. Then, you might no longer have been born. You would suddenly vanish. But much worse than your own suicide, millions, even billions of other people could vanish or never be born in the first place. It's mass murder on a scale that Hitler, Stalin, or Pol Pot could scarcely dream about.

Eryk was interrupted in his thoughts by Dr. Randolph Trice. "Alright, Eryk. Are you with me? Will you do it?"

"What have I got to lose? My life isn't exactly charmed these days and this is the professional opportunity of a lifetime. Most of the historical record is unknown."

It is too true. Despite the authoritative impression conveyed by countless history texts and their accompanying lecturers, historical knowledge is based on the uncertain interpretation of mere scraps of evidence. There are endless mysteries and unknowns in every age and place, conveniently omitted from the historical narrative. Travelling back for a first-hand glimpse would be a fascinating experience for any history buff and a lesson in the effectiveness of historians' reconstruction methods.

"So, you're volunteering? You know this is an experiment to prove the device works. It's not a scholarly historical fact-finding mission so don't treat it like one. You may never come back again. You could suddenly die with no warning."

"I'm ready."

"No, you are not ready. We have to train you first. What you can and can't say and do has to be second nature. It will be drummed into you until it's the only way you think. We can't risk having you destroy the fabric of history. Remember, this is strictly a feasibility test. You're welcome to make a few test observations, but that isn't your purpose. Do you understand that?"

"I realize why I'm going. What I still don't understand is why you don't just send some dust-spec sized cameras, or maybe an insect drone or two, or a micro-recorder."

They were conversing in Trice's plain but tidy office, where every document and note was meticulously filed, stacked, classified, prioritized, and always in its proper place. Trice fit perfectly with his office; he was impeccably dressed in his black dress slacks, plain beige dress shirt and blue tie, solid metal gold-colored glasses, still with a full head of graying hair and not a single strand out of place, his trim and fit fifty-five-year-old frame sitting straight up in his swivel chair.

Eryk with his masculine oblong twenty-eight-year-old face, dark brown hair and strong chin was casual but neat, business informal with his gray slacks and pastel-blue open collar shirt.

"We need to send some intelligence, a person who can judge if anything is going wrong and make immediate adjustments to keep from destroying the future, this future," Trice continued. "Machines can't do that. You are an expert on one of the historical periods that interest us, and that's why I want you to go. I expect you to see at once if events aren't playing out as they should, and do something about it. People are able to sense things and get an intuitive feeling. Machines can't. It's possible that even the act of observation could destroy the future and kill us all."

"Then why do you want me to travel back in time if the present could be suddenly destroyed and you with it?"

"If you are properly and completely trained, if you know exactly what to do in every circumstance, if you know precisely what to look for, and if every step of the operation is rehearsed and verified in advance, then the visit will go precisely as planned. I selected you because I know you're the kind that once you commit to something, you go all out."

"Your machine is dangerous."

"Not in the right hands. Please reflect. What if world leaders could go back and fix their most egregious errors. Neville Chamberlain for example. Think about it."

"You assume their egos will allow them to admit their mistakes and they're dedicated to doing the right things by the institutions they're responsible for. History teaches us neither one is necessarily true. I think we should just be observers, get to real root causes, for example, of the First World War or Great Depression. That's all the machine should allow anyone to do. If we bring back the lessons of history, we can at least hope a few key people will take the lessons seriously for once."

"That's not likely either. People don't venerate the great institutions or the people who built them like they once did. They aren't interested in fixing the flaws and keeping organizations pointed in the direction of the public good. They're only concerned with the big 'me'. The terrorists and malcontents want to destroy what was painstakingly built over the years."

Trice was an order freak. He insisted that everything must be predictable and in its proper preordained place. Life should bear no surprises; he hated the unexpected. He wanted to control every detail, all of it based on the rules. People who acted out their personal whims, anyone who didn't go through channels, and those acted without a documented plan or a list of instructions, none of them deserved a position of authority.

"I scheduled a meeting this morning in the thermodynamics lab with Dauer and Quincy. Do you care to join us there?" Roland Dauer was Trice's chief assistant engineer; Pete Quincy was a physicist specializing in thermodynamics.

"Certainly."

The two of them proceeded to the lab. Just as Trice, Dauer, and Eryk started to talk, Carl Ballo, a technician, was entering the lab with Quincy following directly behind him. Suddenly there was a poppoppop accompanied by a scream. Ballo stumbled into the lab face down, feet in the doorway. Blood gushed from his left leg. Quincy fell backward into the hallway, feet just outside the doorway. Blood spread over the front of his shirt.

With the first pop and scream Dauer ran to the back of the lab. He hid behind one of the giant cooling pumps. Without thinking, Trice grabbed Ballo and pulled him into the lab. At the same time Eryk dropped down on all fours. He leaned out the door and reached under Quincy's back and thighs, carefully pulling him inside amidst blood seeping onto the floor. Their adrenaline surged and spiked. The doorframe popped and cracked as two bullets struck, just missing Trice and Eryk. Trice, his heart pounding audibly, reached up as he sat on the floor and quickly pulled the door closed, locking it in the same motion.

The two of them pulled their charges further from the lab entrance through the spreading blood as another bullet cracked through the middle of the wooden door and zipped between the two of them.

A grimacing Ballo told Trice "Forget me, go hide somewhere and save yourself." Trice ignored him as he yanked off his tie and applied a tight tourniquet to Ballo's leg. A bullet had fractured the bone just above the knee. Blood continued to pour out at an alarming rate until the tourniquet tightened.

Meanwhile Eryk ripped off his shirt and tried to turn it into a pressure bandage to stop the bleeding from the wound on the left side of Quincy's chest. He started CPR. Quincy's pulse was rapidly weakening. Eryk continued mechanically determined not to stop.

The pop-pop-pop continued without letup.

For Quincy, the pain intensified. His face contorted. Both Eryk and Trice noticed the scars and burn marks on his leg, arms, and face.

They heard heavy steps progressing methodically down the hallway; probably Marine guards. After several minutes the shooting stopped. Sirens started to wail from all directions.

Once Ballo was stable and the bleeding was controlled Trice called 911. He sat on the floor and stuck his head out the door. A Marine guard was hurrying down the hall. He saw Trice, and turned around and pointed his rifle directly at Trice's head.

"I'm Dr. Trice. There are two men critically wounded here in the lab. They need immediate medical attention."

Quickly sizing up the situation, the Marine shouldered his rifle and grabbed his mini-walkie-talkie to summon the medics.

Trice ducked back in the lab. "Eryk, would you like me to relieve you with the CPR for a while?"

Eryk's adrenaline was still surging full force. "Not now," he quickly gasped as he kept going.

"How's the pain, Carl?" Trice asked Ballo.

"I'll manage. It hurts a lot but it's nothing like what I went through back in my old country."

Events flew quickly at first, but were now unfolding with agonizing slowness.

"What are you talking about?" Eryk gasped between CPR breaths.

"Randolph knows the story."

Trice stated briefly, "Ballo came here as a political refuge. His parents and brother and sister were all tortured and murdered by a mob bent on ethnic cleansing. He was fortunate to be visiting an uncle but the two of them escaped and came here requesting asylum. He worked menial jobs while he improved his English and put himself through school, worked himself up. It was a struggle for him, but you know how determined he is to be successful."

After about ten minutes three medics arrived in the lab accompanied by two marines. Eryk was still desperately performing CPR though Quincy's pulse had long since stopped.

One medic immobilized Ballo's leg and prepared him for transport. The other two concentrated on Quincy. One of them took over the CPR.

"The bullet struck an artery," the first medic said, referring to Ballo. "This man would have bled to death if you hadn't acted. Now we have to get him to surgery and save the leg." Tending to Quincy, one of the others said, "This man's heart has stopped. There may be brain damage. I think it's too late but we'll keep trying. There might be a chance."

Eryk's face sank with guilt. "I should have done something different. My CPR is too rusty. I could have done more."

"You did everything you could have. It's in the hands of fate," a medic responded.

A Marine said, "We don't know if there are more shooters. We suggest you evacuate the building as soon as we have it secured. One of us will escort you out as soon as it's safe."

Dauer crept out from behind the pump and went up next to the marine, ready to leave.

"Thanks, but I'll get cleaned up and stay," Trice said. "I have work to do. Eryk, why don't you go home and try to relax the rest of the day."

"Alright but I'll be back in as soon as my nerves settle down."

"Stay home. I'll see you first thing tomorrow."

Marines accompanied all of them out when they were ready.

Later, that afternoon, Eryk returned to Trice's office. If nothing else he just needed someone to talk to.

"Eryk, what if you could go back and keep Quincy and Ballo out of the doorway and out of harm's way, even if it was dangerous for you to do it? What if you could have saved the Quincy's life? What if you could go back and arrange for the Marine guards to catch the shooter with the gun before he started his rampage? Would you?"

"Same as you. I don't even have to think about that one."

"I know you wouldn't hesitate. That's what you have the chance to do now, on a much larger scale.

"Imagine how life would be if the terrorists, the con artists, the riot instigators, the drug lords, the murderers and rapists, and the rest of the trouble makers never existed in the first place. Suppose the ones who cause death and destruction and stir people up could be stopped at birth or prevented from being born in the first place? Suppose they couldn't suddenly destroy people's lives with the terrible violence, riots, revolutions, or crime they cause? The world and everyone in it would be so much better off, incredibly better.

"Now do you understand the point of building this time machine? We can stop the really bad people before they inflict harm. If it's within your power to prevent so much suffering, aren't you morally bound to do so? Can you bear the guilt of seeing terrible suffering if you knew you could have stopped it, but instead you stood by and did nothing? I can't and I won't"

* * *

"Why did you say that just watching could be dangerous if it isn't done the right way?"

"You're not a scientist like me, so how could you understand the reason? Quantum physics won't allow you to simply observe. For example, if a single electron (or any other particle or atom or molecule) is sent unobserved through a double slit and onto a screen, it will display a diffraction pattern on the screen as if it was a wave traveling through both slits. If, however, you watch it to see which slit it goes through, it will invariably go through only one slit and land at a single point on the screen. History is altered merely by watching the particle.

"Does this same principle apply to observing the past? Could it be that sending an observer, even a camera and microphone, to merely watch what happened will alter the course of history, just as with the particle? Nobody knows the answer. Theory and experiment have not yet told us what happens on a larger scale."

"Then you're taking a high-risk gamble with the lives of everyone on the planet including some past generations. Shouldn't you wait until you have enough information to prove nothing will go wrong?"

"I'm certain that if you are properly and completely trained, if you know exactly what to do in every circumstance, and if every step of the operation is rehearsed and verified in advance, then the operation will go precisely as planned. I selected you because I know you're the type that once you commit to something, you go all out. There will be rigorous contingency plans covering every uncertainty. You needn't worry if you follow my plan to the letter."

"I don't mean to be difficult, but the world is well beyond complex. According to the theory of non-linear complex systems, there are discontinuities. There are boundaries where things suddenly and drastically change. Once you cross over, there is no going back, no fixing anything. It's like smashing an egg."

"If anything like that happens, I'm certain it will be the result of not maintaining the machine, not staying within the operating parameters at all times. Things will never get to that point."

"Your dedication is most inspiring, but the road to hell is paved with malfunctioning time machines."

"In any case, it doesn't matter. This project has to go forward. The Vice President is taking a personal interest in it. He judges the stakes to be high enough to justify the risk. He's the one who makes sure the project is fully funded, and he makes sure Director Heinrich puts a priority on it. So, this experiment *will* proceed and someone will travel through time whether either of us agrees or not. I'd rather stay in control and guide the effort in a safe direction than turn it over to someone else. How about you?"

"I suppose that would be the wisest course of action."

However, Eryk wasn't so sure about his new role as a caped superhero traveling back in time to excise all evil from the world, overcoming all manner of sinister superhuman maniacal villains and nuclear fire-breathing mutant dragons to make the world a better place. But Trice was right that they should not risk losing control of the machine. Besides, any historian worthy of the label dreamt of seeing history in person exactly as really was, not as it was reconstructed by scholars.

Eryk's specialty was American history between the Civil War and the First World War. He had an unbelievable opportunity to not only see it, but to personally experience it exactly as it was.

"I'm glad you agree with me," Trice stated. "We have to find someone to exchange you with."

"What are you talking about? That's something you've never mentioned before."

"Laws of physics. I'll brief you later."

What if, Eryk thought, he went back in history merely as an observer and then returned? Suppose he did in fact accidentally alter history? My god, everything he knew about history would be wrong! He could no longer teach or write papers about it. What would he do for a living then?

* * *

Juanita Heller was an aggressive political climber, and she set her sights on a deputy director position at the Agency. Whatever her bosses demanded she went one step beyond, that is, if she could prevent them from taking credit for her work and bargain for her own share of the glory. However, if she expected a supervisor to take credit for her work, as was common in a politically-driven organization, her work would be intentionally sloppy, which left her with a clean reputation and her boss with egg on his face. She also saw to it that her share of the credit was suitably embellished, and she took the kudos for others' contributions when she could get away with it.

All of this was well understood; it was standard office politics. Everyone with any ambition at all played the same game with a straight face, pretending as if politics was not driving the show.

Trice assigned Heller to do detailed mission planning and oversee staff, and in particular, time-traveler training and preparation. He was smart enough to know that if he gave her full public credit, he would get her best effort and gain an ally besides.

Eryk's professional ambition was the study of history and the lessons to be learned from that. Heller understood he was no threat to her and, in fact, the situation was ideal. She would make sure everyone knew that if he screwed the mission up, well then, it was his incompetence. After all, she did everything she could. If Eryk was successful, it was all on account of her superb preparation, research, and training; the brilliant execution of the plan was entirely due to her. In other words, she knew how to play the game.

* * *

Dauer interrupted Trice and Eryk with one of his many petty personal issues.

"Trice," he complained, "You know Dauer has a master's degree in physics from an Ivy League school and knows every technical detail about your time machine and your scientific breakthroughs it's based on. You know his master's thesis was on the granularity of space and time and how they are interrelated so that the shrinkage of one means the expansion of the other."

Dauer always referred to himself in the third person.

"Everyone in this agency knows that nobody, not even you, can devote full attention to both technical research and development and to administrative duties at the same time, and everyone agrees you should focus on the administrative details and hand over technical leadership to your deputy engineer Mr. Dauer," Dauer continued.

"Roland, I've never really heard that opinion from anyone else but you."

"That's because they don't want to upset you, but when you have such a brilliant deputy engineer don't you think it's wise to make full use of him?" Clearly, Dauer lacked the political skills of a Heller. This was just another of his endless lame attempts to take charge of the time machine project.

"I don't trust anyone else on this project to be as detailed as I am, including you, and mismanaging the details on a project like this could be catastrophic. Besides, I've already assigned you to solve the most visible problem I have, the one that will get you noticed and promoted if that's what you want. If you come through, I promise you full credit."

"But Dauer should be working on the machine itself. He wastes his talent working on other things," Dauer countered.

"Roland, it is a vital to the machine and it's is no small thing. Director Heinrich has made a really big deal out of it. You'll get a lot of recognition. I'm counting on you."

"Dauer says the heat problem is an annoyance because it doesn't affect the workings of the machine or the details of the mission."

"To the higher-ups it's the most important concern of them all next to seeing the machine work. You should be happy you were assigned the problem and I expect you to take care of it in a timely manner."

"But it's a thermodynamics problem and it's not the central apparatus," Dauer persisted. "Mr. Dauer is a physicist and he should be focused on the essential mechanisms."

"What problem are you talking about?" Eryk interrupted.

"Warping space-time for time travel requires focusing a huge amount of energy into a small space in order to invert space and time for a brief period that is nevertheless long enough to travel through," Trice explained. "By the laws of thermodynamics, no machine can ever be a hundred percent efficient. That means a great deal of waste heat will be generated whenever we use the machine.

"The Director and the Vice President have placed a high priority on this project and made it top secret. I don't think that the President even knows about it. But, every time we fire up the machine, every weather and spy satellite over North America sees an enormous flash of heat, then the heat generates brief, sudden local thunderstorms and a rush of wind, and there's a widespread twominute brownout everywhere east of the Mississippi. Lots of people are asking a lot of questions as you know. The powers that be are demanding we find a heat sink immediately and they're demanding we finish the design and construction of a mega power source that can use the same heat sink. The Vice President is especially adamant that nobody infers the existence of this project."

"Then why don't you find a team of thermodynamics guys to hurry up with a solution?" Dauer interrupted.

"That's what I assigned you to do," Trice answered. "I need to get these people off my back. Do you think you can move a little faster on it? I consider you the best man for the job."

"The problem is beneath Mr. Dauer's capabilities. Mr. Dauer demands more important work on the guts of the machine itself." Dauer refused to drop the subject.

"Then the sooner you solve this problem the sooner you will get the work you want. I will make you that promise."

This was not the outcome Dauer wanted. He decided to trot down the hall and press his case with Heller.

Dauer was a relentless self-promoter who had risen up through the bureaucracy to his current modest position by working his supervisors until they were fed up with him and sent him up the chain to get rid of him. Trice had not chosen Dauer as his assistant, but made the best use of him he could.

"Everybody thinks Trice is such a genius but Mr. Dauer is just as good a scientist and engineer," Dauer complained to Heller. "He has learned every essential principle about how the machine works, how it's designed, and how it was built, and he can do anything Trice can do. Anyone in this Agency who thinks about it would say that Mr. Dauer should take over the technical work and leave Trice to handle administrative details."

"That's certainly something to think about," Heller humored him. She figured that maybe she could make use of Dauer and dangle what he wanted like a carrot in front of his nose. If he did in fact know enough and wasn't just bragging again, she thought, maybe she could use him to push Trice out or get him transferred or demoted, then she could move into his position. The time machine project had the attention of the Director after all, and control of it could even be a ticket to her own directorship. She would string Dauer along until she knew. She called research assistant Sandy Watkins.

"Sandy, I have a job for you."

"Great. I'm always happy to help out."

"Keep an eye on Dauer, see what Trice tells him to do, and whether he is capable and finishes his work on time and without mistakes. Don't tell anybody you're doing it. I need an objective evaluation. Will you do that for me?"

"Sure. I'll tell you everything I find out."

* * *

"What do you mean you are going to exchange me with someone else?" Eryk asked Trice. "I'm not sure I can accept that."

"Relax. You will still retain your own consciousness. After a while I will bring you back and reverse the exchange so we can evaluate the experiment. It's all a matter of physics. The second law of thermodynamics says that entropy must become larger over time. In other words, disorder has to increase on the whole. If we just send you back suddenly, you will instantly decrease the entropy of the time and that would violate the laws of nature. If we tried it, I'm sure it would kill you. There has to be an exchange with no net alteration in the disorder of either the past or the present."

My God Eryk thought, Trice doesn't realize it's a symmetrical situation. The exchanged person can't change history when he returns his previous time any more than Eryk can. He can't take any knowledge of the future he has glimpsed back with him. However, he could change the present without killing anyone, in fact, he could easily change Eryk's future. What will this someone do to his life in his absence? That part isn't symmetrical. Eryk could return as a pariah and never know why.

Chapter Two
History

"I don't know why Trice picked *you* to go," Heller complained to Eryk. "You're too bookish and impractical. You can't control people and you have no political consciousness. You're not the right type to be a time traveler. If there's a problem, you'll waste precious time reflecting on it. I should be the one who decides on the time traveler. It calls for someone like me. Trice just doesn't get it."

"Talk to him then. I trust him. I'll abide by whatever he says."

"Trice is a throwback. His time came and went before he was ever born. He thinks he has to have some higher purpose. That's an expensive ambition. He thinks he has to follow some supposed moral principles he conjured up from who knows where, but it's all nonsense."

"At least his principles don't change every time he gets a better offer."

"You're no better than he is."

"What was that attack all about yesterday, anyway?"

"Some crazy contractor smuggled in some ammunition, then he 3D printed two semi-automatic handguns with the Agency's own printers. I heard he murdered three and wounded five more before the marines shot him."

* * *

Besides being an administrator, Heller herself was an amateur history buff, which was one reason she was assigned to the project under Trice in the first place, and one reason Trice assigned her to handle Eryk.

"Why did you specialize in the progressive period of American history?" Heller asked. She figured Eryk's class lecture would surely follow.

"These days everybody thinks the close of the twentieth century and the beginning of the twenty-first is an era of great change, especially because of computerization, innovation, the explosion of social media and herding behavior, instant communications, and the greater speed things happen at, but the period from about 1893 up through the Great Depression was even more dynamic. Technological and social change was even more dramatic than it has been recently."

Most of the important technological innovations that transformed everyone's life were introduced during this period. That included the commercialization of electricity; the first practical light bulb in 1879, city lighting in the 1880s, practical storage batteries and dry cells, the beginnings of the electric grid along with home and factory electric service which meant appliance and industrial equipment could be placed anywhere; appliances like the dishwasher, the vacuum cleaner in 1899, air conditioners in 1902, and numerous others were invented and commercialized.

There were revolutionary transportation and communication breakthroughs such as the first powered flight in 1903, the telephone in 1876, radio in 1895 with the first transatlantic radio broadcast in 1901, automobiles in the 1890s and the Ford Model T in 1908, steamships and the end of the age of sail, city-wide subway systems, electric trams and streetcars within and between cities in the late 1880s, the simple box camera in 1888, movies in 1903 and talkies in 1910, and the phonograph with wax cylinders in 1877 and audio disks in the 1890s.

It was an age of invention and there were many new developments great and small, such as indoor plumbing, the modern assembly line patented and used by Ransom Olds in 1901 and automated by Henry Ford in 1913, the elevator brake allowing tall buildings to be constructed, the tractor in 1892 and the practical farm tractor in 1904 allowing greater farm productivity, synthetic plastic in 1907, and modern steel production, not to mention necessities like instant coffee. By the first decade of the new century, roughly twentyfive per cent of households had flush toilets, five per cent had clothes washers, and three per cent had electric refrigerators. Many households owned a sewing machine, often mechanically operated by a pedal or a hand crank.

Major social changes inevitably followed. There was a widespread migration from the farms to the cities. The frontier vanished in the 1890s although there were still some hotspots for westward migration. With no more free land, an escape valve closed tight and some people thought America would become petrified like Europe, a sorry state in their mind.

However, this fossilization of America, the casting in concrete of the status quo many philosophers feared at the time, wouldn't happen for another century. Instead, a new dynamism emerged. Many people worried that traits demanded by the frontier that made Americans what they were, such as self-reliance, equality, resourcefulness, seizing of abundant opportunity, and optimism would disappear with the frontier except in myth. As it happened, it took another hundred years for this loss of optimism and self-reliance to germinate, but traditional, that is to say rural, values *did* start disappearing along with the frontier and the rapid expansion of the cities.

Americans came to believe in progress and in a brighter future for every new generation.

The industrialization that gained traction with the Civil War accelerated in the 1890s and continued gaining momentum thereafter, forcing ever increasing urbanization. Cities expanded rapidly, though the transition would not be completed until at least World War II. The social and economic buffer of small community and farm life that got people through hard times was vanishing as a result and was nowhere to be found in the impersonal cities.

The rise of the tycoon and the benefits and evils this spawned continued and were fait accompli. However, especially during the panic of 1893 to 1897, financial power transitioned from the Rockefellers, Vanderbilts, Goulds, and Carnegies to financiers like J. P. Morgan and to foreign and domestic speculators, where power became highly concentrated.

Giant corporations and trusts still had a major influence, but the concentration of economic power in the hands of bankers, financiers and speculators is a situation that not only still persists to this day, but has intensified. The result was noticeably less security and more anxiety.

Daily strife increased a great deal, especially in the cities. Rapid industrialization and immigration made cities nearly ungovernable, amplified traditional endemic American corruption and nepotism, and strengthened political machines such as Tammany Hall and the Daley machine. Labor became well-organized. Strikes and violent unrest and confrontations between labor and management mushroomed. Giant corporations and financial institutions sometimes exerted a stranglehold on labor. Class disparities and privilege became the subject of envy as much as it had previously been an object of admiration and a goal to struggle towards. Political agitation and the Progressive movement gained a widespread following. Both demagogues and reformers flourished.

Living standards changed for both better and worse. Three quarters of city dwellers lived in crowded, filthy, disease-ridden rental housing, particularly immigrants assimilating from all over the world. Pessimists, and there were more than a few, were convinced economic hardship and corruption was the future and America was plunging over a cliff, while optimists thought the American spirit would somehow triumph in the end.

Overall, most ordinary Americans, and especially the immigrants, had this sense of optimism, and thought that the future would be decidedly different and better, and it was a future they would have the opportunity to participate in themselves. Indeed, Alexander Graham Bell, Nicola Tesla, Andrew Carnegie, and many other key contributors to the modern world were American immigrants.

During the ten-week Spanish-American War of 1898, pushed by the expansionists and manifest destiny seekers, the U.S. was instantly thrust from an isolationist preoccupation with parochial national affairs to international responsibilities. Worldwide territories brought worldwide concerns. It was at this time that the United States became a world power, intervening more and more into foreign countries' affairs. Big stick diplomacy came to the fore.

Other events shaped the times, such as the panics of 1893 and October 1907, the 1893 Columbian Exhibition (in honor of the 400th anniversary of the discovery of America), the 1906 San Francisco earthquake, and the establishment of numerous new Federal bureaucracies.

There were proud new American cultural achievements. The U.S. began exporting its culture rather than reflecting that of Europe and others. American jazz, American movies, Wild West shows, and other American arts became popular in other countries. That included newly invented food products such as Hershey bars, Hershey Kisses, animal crackers, self-rising flour, Baked Beans, Planters Nuts, corn flakes, and hot fudge sundaes.

This era was also a psychological battleground, a battle between inner forces and external temptations, between intense and contradictory shadow forces that the big and persistent changes evoked in the unconscious, and between greed, altruism, reform and the new organizations each of these spawned. It is no coincidence that the greatest advances in the foundations of psychology were forged during this period by Wundt, Pavlov, James, Freud, Jung, and others.

Modern manipulative advertising based on Freudian psychology very naturally came of age at this time starting in America, as the transition began to a much more consumer-oriented society.

New institutions and super-sized old institutions sprung up whole: department stores; skyscrapers; newly accessible parks and amusements; and sporting events such as the World Series, the Davis Cup, the Rose Bowl, and automobile races erupted right and left.

Altogether, it was an era of great upheaval, transition, and change. All of these new forces acting on everyday life were overwhelming and simply staggering. A long and difficult transition period from the rural to the modern era gathered force in the 1890s, interrupted and influenced by World War I, continuing through the Roaring 20s, hijacked by the Great Depression, and finally completed with the outbreak of World War II. This is where and when the foundation of the twentieth and twenty-first centuries was forged.

The dynamism, optimism, technological and cultural progress, and increasing affluence of the period are mesmerizing.

Eryk concluded, "This was the second of the three great transitions of the human species. The first was the transition from hunting/gathering to an agrarian, rural agricultural lifestyle. Mass industrialization and urbanization was the second. The third and future transformation will be the colonization of space. I hope I'm around to record that one, but I fear it may not be in the cards."

He was licking his chops to go see this dynamic era for himself.

Chapter Three
The Reception

"You were just an accident, a mistake, a flirtation that got out of hand." Natalie Samicki's evening rant was directed, as usual, at her husband Eryk. "Now you're an albatross. I absolutely despise you. What are you good for anyway? I'm embarrassed to introduce you to my friends, you're just too boring. History, baseball, piano, who cares about that? You don't even watch TV, you just read dull books about stupid old stuff, so how can you ever know what anyone else talks about? For God's sake, you don't even know what the latest shows and movies are. You never heard of half the celebrities people watch or what everybody says about them. Who's going to want to talk to you anyway? Not me, that's for sure."

"Hon, you know I love you and variety is the spice of life."

"You're no good to me. If you want to keep me you better change, as in immediately! If it wasn't for you, I'd be with a man who was rich and famous right now, living in a mansion, driving a Mercedes, wearing the finest designer clothes, having anything I wanted. But look what happened. Is your precious history going to get me what I want? You're just a big waste of my time."

Natalie was a classic beauty, five and a half feet tall sans shoes, blonde, blue-eyed, with a magnificent roundish face men couldn't help drooling over, full pouting lips, long legs, and ample curves in all the right places, a complete femme fatale. But looks are no more than half of what makes up a femme fatale. Dress and makeup, accentuating what you have and minimizing what you don't are, of course, vital. Projecting the aura of a bedroom virtuoso and that it's her favorite place in the entire world to be (even though that's quite often a deception), and a glance that says "I want you, try to catch me" are an essential part of the package. The ambitious femme fatale must pay attention to the three B's: bedroom, bankroll, and boardroom.

Eryk's wife had it all. She certainly dressed the part with her low-cut blouses, short skirts and platform heels.

He fell right into her trap. The problem was, she was playing catch and release and he didn't release.

* * *

Vice President Bentler figured it was about time to talk face to face with some of the characters at the spook agency so he could size them up. He needed to be ready with a plan when his time came to move. He called the agency Director in the latter's spacious, wellfurnished corner office at the Agency.

"Heinrich, I need to talk to you and your deputy directors face to face in an informal setting. I want you to call an internal reception, no outsiders, no publicity, and no congressmen or staffers, strictly agency only. All personal invitations and no announcements. Spouses are invited so I can meet them, too, and see what *they* want. Make sure there's an unlimited open bar. Everything on a strict need-to-know basis." Plentiful booze might encourage the marks to let their guards down.

* * *

"Dear," Eryk asked Natalie that evening once she was finished putting him in his place, "the Director asked me to attend an agency reception tomorrow afternoon. You're invited, too. I would like it if you came with me."

"Honestly, you're not worth the trouble."

"Please? I heard the Vice President might be there."

"Alright, I suppose it might be interesting to see some of the losers you hang out with."

"Thank you, dear. Can you dress conservatively? It's a business environment."

She responded sarcastically, "Just for you, I'll wear a *dark* red miniskirt this time."

They both knew Eryk didn't mean it. He was proud of his wife's beauty and liked to show off his prize. The next afternoon she showed up at the security gate wearing a dark red frilly blouse with a plunging, actually cliff-diving, neckline, an off-white miniskirt, her gaudiest platform heels, and her best bling.

* * *

Nobody missed Natalie's grand entrance, that is, none of the men. Some watched from the corner of their eye, some stared and didn't bother to hide the fact, some pretended not to look, but none failed to notice. Wives made every attempt to be sure their husbands' attention was riveted to the back of the room. Natalie's entrance was a glorious contrast to the windowless plain beige interior government meeting room with the open bar in the middle, a few scattered chairs and hors d'oeuvres tables around the periphery, assorted pictures of wooden-faced directors, vice presidents, and presidents scattered about the walls, and standard ceiling tiles with round light fixtures among the recording cameras that looked like light fixtures, watching carefully and taking their digital notes.

Meanwhile, Vice President Bentler immediately sought out Director Heinrich at the reception.

"Heinrich, when will that damned time machine be ready? You've been working on if for four years and you promised I would have it by now. My term expires in another two years and I don't have time to wait for it, so what the hell is the hold up?"

"I think it's almost ready, I mean if no serious glitches turn up.

Dr. Trice is doing the final testing now. He plans a couple of test trips to the past with full evaluations of the results. He'll adjust his procedures and tune up the operating parameters, then I understand it should be ready."

"If you want to keep your job it *will* be ready. Otherwise, you'll be on the street and nobody will hire you for dog catcher in this town. I want to use it within the next six months, is that clear? Take any short cuts you have to."

"It's up to Dr. Trice to say when it's ready. He's the only one who can judge."

"What is this 'Dr. Trice' bullshit? That's all I hear from everybody. Doesn't he work for you? Can't you even control your own people?"

"He's the genius who invented the machine and nobody else really understands the principles behind it the way he does."

"So, then what happens if he gets run over by a bus? What happens if some private outfit makes him an offer he can't refuse? Do you have any contingency plans?"

"Well, I've thought about that some."

"You've 'thought about it some'? What kind of sloppy director are you, anyway? Why haven't you found some other expert to learn everything about Trice's work so they can take over if they have to? What if Trice turns uncooperative?"

"There's nobody else I know of who's brilliant enough to understand it, though we do have someone named Dauer who claims he knows how it works."

"And have you verified this Dauer character's claims? Have you set up a schedule so he can learn every aspect of the machine? Have you required Trice to write everything down, to document what he's doing?"

"Trice says he doesn't have time to write things down or else the program will fall behind schedule. He keeps everything in his head."

"I can't believe what you're telling me! All you hand me are excuses. I expect you to shape up and get control of your project! I'm going to monitor your activities closely from now on. This project is my highest priority, and heads will roll if it isn't ready when I want it, including yours, is that understood?"

"Yes, Mr. Vice President, you can trust me to see to it."

Bentler determined to talk to this Dauer character and find out what he really knew. He told Heinrich to point him out.

"Dauer, you claim to be an expert on Trice's time machine. Is that correct?" Bentler asked him.

"Yes, sir, Dauer should be the one running the project. Dr. Trice is spread too thin and he should just focus on administrative matters," Dauer sensed the golden opportunity to press his case.

"Do you know enough to document how the machine works, in detail?"

"Yes, Dauer believes so," he replied hesitantly. It wasn't a convincing answer.

"Then why haven't you? I understand Trice claims he doesn't have the time to write anything down. Somebody has to. I want you to write down everything there is to know about how the time machine works and how to operate it and send it to me. This is a secret order. Do it in your spare time and don't tell anyone about it. And I mean absolutely nobody. Can you follow my simple orders?" "Yes, sir," Dauer replied in a shaky voice.

Meanwhile, Juanita Heller was in full observation mode. Was anybody important going to compromise themselves and give her something to use against them? She paid particular attention to the open bar. Was anyone getting drunk? Did anyone have enough to drink to loosen their tongue? Who was spending inordinate amounts of time talking to whom? Who was tight with whom? She herself would not drink anything other than the few sips it might take to encourage her prey of the moment to drink more and loosen their lips.

She noticed Dauer's conversation with Bentler. He had had a lot to drink already. "What did Bentler want?" she asked him.

"I'm not supposed to tell you. He's in a hurry to finish the machine."

"What else?"

"He asked me if Dauer knows how it works."

"Do you?"

"Of course. Dauer knows all about it."

"Is that what you told him?"

"What else did you expect Dauer to say?"

"What did he tell you to do?"

"Dauer isn't allowed to say."

"I see. Did you say you like dry martinis? Have another drink with me."

Director Heinrich was also spending a lot of time at the bar. He also talked to Bentler, and Heller wanted to know what kind of plans they were making together. She worked her way over to him.

"Bentler takes quite an interest in the agency, doesn't he? Did he give you any priorities I should know about?"

"He wants the time machine finished in six months. You'd better be on top of it."

"Does anyone brief you about the progress?"

"Things bubble up through the chain. I get executive summaries."

"I'll bet all anyone tells you is what they think you want to hear. Their advancement depends on your good opinion. I could be a big help to you. Don't you think you need the real story?"

"Look, I'm a very busy man. I can't get into the details about every little thing. I have staff to take care of that."

"What if your boss or his boss, the Secretary of Defense, or the Vice President, wants the details? Bentler is talking directly to you. The Secretary of Defense isn't here, so he wants something from you."

"Yeah, I know, but I can always get one of my staff to write a report. Why are you so inquisitive about it, anyway?"

"It appears obvious to me you need more timely information if you want to satisfy Bentler."

"Bentler's not my boss, the secretary is. As long as I get good information in my weekly briefings that's good enough."

"You're hopeless. Don't you think Bentler talks to the secretary himself? How does it look if Bentler is on top of things in your department but you aren't?"

"I'm not worried about it."

"Why don't you let me give you regular briefings, off the record, of course? That way you'll be prepared if Bentler comes directly to you for a progress report instead of going through the secretary."

"I'm sorry, my head is spinning. This is a party for heaven's sake. Can we talk about this some other time?"

"As you wish."

"I'll contact you when I'm ready."

"Make it soon."

Natalie glanced halfway across the room, making eye contact with Trice for a second before she looked down at her plunging red neckline and flipped her hair. She would continue to look the other way for a few minutes until she accidently almost tripped over his shuffling frame. "Oh! Please excuse me! You must be the Dr. Trice Eryk is always talking about. He says you're the biggest genius on earth. I'm sure that isn't your only talent, either."

Trice flushed red and stammered, "You're Natalie?"

"Yes, and very pleased to meet you. What is this secret project

Eryk won't tell me about? Oops! I'm so clumsy! I dropped my cracker. Could you possibly be a gentleman and get me another one?"

"Certainly."

Charmingly naïve, she thought. Of course, when Trice came back, she was gone.

Natalie glanced in the direction of Dauer, licking her lips and very deliberately withdrawing her gaze when he noticed it. Then she disappeared into the crowd for a few minutes before enacting a repeat performance. He wasted no time looking for, and directly approaching her.

"Who are you? You look like someone important. Are you the Vice President?" Natalie inquired.

"Almost. I'm Roland Dauer. Dauer is the brains behind a topsecret project of the highest priority," he continued.

"I don't have time to be bored to death," Natalie thought to herself. "Please excuse me," she muttered as she slinked away.

Meanwhile, it was time for Bentler to confront Heller and give her some direction.

"Heller, I see you have ambitions. You will be my eyes and ears on this project, understand? Tell me, does anyone control Trice? Who decides on the schedule? What is the real status of the machine? I want to know what is going on, and I mean what is *really* going on. Can I depend on you?"

"I assure you Mr. Bentler, from now on it will be my highest priority to find out everything that's going on and to let you know. Trice calls the shots because nobody else understands the entire machine and its principles, only bits and pieces. Nobody dares to replace him or tell him what to do."

"That's intolerable. Someone else, someone I can trust, someone I can control, has to be able to take over the project if that proves necessary."

"I'm working on that, Mr. Bentler."

"I'll bet you are." It takes on piranha to know another. "Will Trice make his schedule?"

"I don't know. Nobody does. I can tell you he's dedicated his heart and soul to his machine and he will do absolutely anything to make it work. My fear is that he will be like some mad inventors who keep tinkering with their inventions trying to make them perfect and never finishing them as a result. I don't think Trice will do that, but he's extremely meticulous and won't release his machine unless the outcome from using it is one hundred per cent predictable."

"I need more precise information than that."

"I'll make a report with everything I know and make discrete inquiries among Trice's key engineering staff. I can put it in a format with an executive summary, a narrative, supplemental details, and key issues and variables for you. Let me be frank, as a supporter of yours, if I do a good job for you, I expect you to keep me in mind for an important position later."

"I see. That's how you roll. Let me see how valuable your work is to me. If the machine isn't ready soon, I may have to seize it and use it anyway. I need capable people who are prepared to operate it for me. I want you to identify those people so I make certain they're prepared, right now."

"Yes, sir, I totally understand what you want."

"I expect you to prove to me that I can rely on you implicitly. If you have grander ideas of your own, you'd better drop them right now."

"Don't even worry about that. As far as I'm concerned you are my real director. I think we understand each other."

Bentler unconsciously sensed in Heller a corrupt ambition that would stop at nothing to get what it wanted and rationalize an excuse for anything she did in the service of that ambition. It was a trait he well recognized, but despised and feared in others. She was someone to be used and immediately disposed of as soon as he no longer needed her. He, of course, presented a façade of having better principles and would never be so ruthless himself.

Heller, for her part, had a vague feeling that Bentler possessed an unquenchable lust for power and a limitless greed for everything material with no discernable limits. She certainly had her own moral foundation, and she pretended would never stoop to Bentler's low level. He was simply a set of coat tails she could hitch a ride on, but at some point, he would cease to be useful and become a threat. She would be forced to permanently, publicly humble or neutralize him, and she already had an idea about how to do it.

This was a classic case of the pot calling the kettle black and vice versa, while they both imagined they were themselves polished bronze containers. It all took place at a visceral level, avoiding the danger of having to face any conscious awareness about themselves. Only one of the two of them was likely survive in the end. Which of the two would prove the most skilled at this high-stakes game? Natalie started smoothing her short skirt and looking at Watkins out of the corner of her eye as he walked past. "Don't I know you?" she said quietly.

He paused. "Well, um, I work at the agency," he stammered.

"Do you know Eryk Samicki?" She asked in a meek little voice.

"Yes, I ah work with him sometimes."

"Is it interesting work you do?" she said as she got up and sauntered towards the bar.

"Yes, um, I think so. Can I maybe ah get you a drink?" Watkins asked, following her like a puppy dog. This was just too easy. Time to move on.

"Don't worry about it," Natalie said in a normal tone of voice as she changed direction. "Have you seen the director? Never mind, I see him," she said as she again disappeared into the crowd.

"Ms. Heller, I saw Eryk's wife coming on to Trice," Watkins reported. "Do you think anything is going on between them?" "Eryk's wife comes on to everything that wears pants. Always looking for her best offer for the moment. I don't think Trice has time for anything but his machine."

"I don't like her. Should I keep an eye on them for you?"

"Please do. I also want you to report to me anything Trice does that isn't in his project plan that you happen to see. Tell me about any unexpected results, and anything new he asks you to do. Can I count on you?"

"I'll do my best."

"Good. I know you're someone I can always count on."

Natalie spotted a sharply dressed average looking man trailing behind Heller. As soon as he glanced around the room, she seized the opportunity to blow him a kiss. He quickly jerked his eyes back and bore them straight into the back of Heller's head. Did he somehow think he could get away with that kind of behavior she wondered?

Her opportunity came soon enough when he walked over to the bar, two drinks in hand ready for refills.

"Hey, handsome. You avoiding me?" she said.

A nervous David Heller responded, "I'm sorry, did I hurt your feelings?"

"Yes, you certainly did. Why don't you make it up to me and fetch me a fresh drink?"

"I'm sorry, my wife will kill me if she sees me talking to another woman," he said, visibly nervous. "I have to go." Then he scurried off.

By now it was high time for Bentler to have a "heart-to-heart" talk with Trice, the key to the project that so interested him. He spotted Trice and went directly to him.

"Trice, when will your machine be ready to use? I want a simple direct answer to my question."

"I think in another six months to a year. Depends on whether there are any new bugs or unexpected side effects."

"I want it in six months, and I want you to give me a firm commitment, do you understand that?"

"I understand what you want, but please keep in mind that using a time machine can have dangerous, destructive, unintended consequences. There have to be foolproof safeguards before the machine can be used."

"Then I expect you to have all of the problems solved in six months' time. Cut the testing short or whatever else you have to do. This is your baby. If I fire you, you'll never see it to completion, so I expect you to play ball. If it isn't ready when I want it, I'll cut you loose and you'll never see it finished."

"I already understand it's a high priority. I must do my job to the highest professional and scientific standards." "Just hurry it up. I'll be watching closely." Bentler went for another drink.

Of course, Natalie caught the eye of Bentler from the start. She had returned to the bar and Bentler took her aside.

"Do you know who I am?" he asked.

"You're Vice President Bentler!" Natalie gasped as she feigned shock and awe. "Imagine me, just simple little me, introduced to the Vice President! It's an honor I could never imagine being worthy of," she said in a low distant voice as she delicately bowed her head in the direction of her ample silicone cleavage while still managing a glance upward into his dark, impenetrable eyes. Truly it would be her ultimate conquest to capture Bentler's interest she thought.

"Who are you again?" Bentler asked.

"My husband works for Doctor Trice and Miss Heller at the Agency."

Bentler's budding disinterest started to dissipate. "And what does your husband say about his work?" he inquired. Maybe she had some information he would find useful.

"Oh, he won't tell me anything. He says his project is top secret and he can't talk about it."

"I see. Please excuse me, I have to talk to the Director right now." There would be nothing useful from this source.

Eryk drank only soft drinks. No loose tongue there. Heller approached him. "Eryk, doesn't it embarrass you the way your wife mixes with all of the men here but she never talks to you?"

"I just try to understand her needs the best I can."

"Aren't you going to do something about it? Are you some kind of masochist that you want her to treat you like that?"

"No, I want her to change. Someday she will realize what she does."

Heller thought, this was a tough case. He was too introverted and a bit of a boy scout. He listened to what other people had to say and weighed it, but then he made his own decision. How would she corrupt or manipulate someone like that? Well, she would come up with a way. He didn't drink or have any of the usual vices. Yet there might come a time when Trice sent him back in his machine but she wanted him to carry out *her* agenda, not Trice's or the agency's program. Blackmail must be the way to go, a way to maneuver him into some violation. She would find some secret or personal quirk, or at least create some compromising appearance. Natalie looked to be his biggest vulnerability.

"Eryk, nothing is going to change unless you force it to."

"What expect me to do? If I press her, she'll just leave and there won't be any chance left to fix things. I just do what I can and wait for a day when she'll come around. One day maybe she will learn to value me."

"I don't see any change in that direction. Quite the opposite. Just look at her. Has she been by your side even once since you both walked through the door?"

After sizing up her prospects it looked to Natalie like Trice was the least dull in the field of uninspiring game pieces. She went up behind him and "accidentally" brushed his shoulder, her hand barely sweeping the back of his waist. "Oh! Excuse me again!" Natalie said softly. "It seems our paths are destined to cross. Eryk tells me you're an expert at destiny, past and present," she giggled as she slowly swept some imaginary dust from her left shoulder.

"Seems so," Trice responded.

Natalie was finished with her explorations and ready to leave. She gave Trice a wink over her shoulder as she grabbed Eryk and left the party.

On the way home a sloshed Natalie vented on Eryk. "Look at you! I'll bet you didn't talk to anyone about anything except your precious history. Did anybody want to talk about that? No, of course not. I'm sure everyone ran away. Did you have a drink with anyone? No, of course not. I'll bet you didn't enjoy yourself for one second. What's the point of you coming to a party like this anyway? None, there isn't any. You just embarrass me and you don't even care. You can't compromise your stupid interests and mix like everyone else. You make me ashamed of you.

"Why don't you just go to a historical convention where you can have a ball? You're not fit to hang out with ordinary people. I don't know what to do with you. I tell you how to dress, what to say, what your interests should be, how to be sociable, and I try so hard to help you out, but do you listen? Do you take my advice? No, no way. You're as determined as ever to dig in and be your same old stupid, boring self that everybody wants to avoid. You drive me to seek interesting company with other men, then you complain about it but it's all your fault. I try, heaven knows how hard I try with you, but you never listen..."

* * *

Eryk felt like a country singer. His dog died, his wife ran away, and his pickup broke down. How could it get any worse than that? If the machine failed during his time travel and he ended up in limbo or even dead he almost didn't care anymore.

Now, Eryk mused, he understood clearly how one partner in a relationship could drive the other to drink or even to suicide. But what was he thinking? He didn't think he would ever become that desperate.

Besides, he had other options he thought. Why not go back in history to Lynchburg, Virginia where her family was from and just stop a romantic encounter by one of her ancestors so she was never born? Or better yet, arrange for Natalie to meet Bentler and the two of them get married. That would be so delicious! The two of them deserved each other. Would it be so bad after all?

* * *

As a newly minted history PhD specializing in the Gilded Age and the Progressive Era of American history, Eryk expected a tough road looking for a teaching job. He expected a multi-year stint as a post doc, or maybe he would find a low-level teaching job, doing research and trying to get published in some respected journal on the side. Either way, he thought he would have to try to climb to a more prestigious position where he could pursue his interest in America's transition to the modern age.

Instead, he was surprised to be recruited by a spy agency. What could they possibly want with him? At least it was a job and he had no other immediate prospect, so he took it. It turned out to be the most interesting and challenging career he could have chosen.

Besides history, Eryk's passions were music and baseball, and he loved to play both. On the diamond, he wanted to pitch. His arsenal consisted of a change-up and a split-fingered fastball. Actually, it was more of a split-fingered medium ball, so he tried to compensate by always aiming for one of the corners of the strike zone. Sometimes that worked, more often it was a disaster, but he was always eager to try again.

Musically, he was a highly talented pianist, ready to plunk away from memory on any piano he happened to pass by, for fun and to keep in practice.

Now Eryk had arrived at the point where he wanted some peace. He wanted to get away, maybe even somehow find a niche somewhere in history to start a new and better life without changing the course of the world. That would also satisfy his urge to explore history. He didn't dare express this sentiment to anyone, otherwise they would consider him to be too dangerous to remain on the project.

* * *

Eryk phoned his wife from his cramped but reasonably neat interior office.

"I'm sorry, dear, but I'll be a little late getting home. I have something to finish up before I can leave."

"Is that all you think about, your precious work? I should be your highest priority. Why aren't you here to entertain me? You always leave me alone like this. Doesn't that bother you?"

"OK, you're right. I'll leave now."

"Don't worry about it. I know how you are. This is the way you treat me. Just do what you have to and I'll see you when you get here."

What, that's all? Eryk was expecting a lot more criticism than that. He didn't know what to make of it.

Eryk was working late but he wasn't studying scenarios and scripts for his upcoming time travel. He was busy looking up and memorizing his wife's family tree.

Chapter Four
Preparation

Could they pull it off? It was the beginning of a new era, like the first powered flight or the first sub-orbital flight of the moon landing program, and just as risky.

"How do you know you've thought of everything?" Eryk questioned. "I'm nervous, aren't you?"

"This is a step-by-step operation, just like the moon landing," Trice responded. They were again in his office going over Trice's latest plan. "We're proving each small step before we go on to the next. I have every confidence in the program. Before the first moon landing, they tested and proved every piece of equipment and every single step on the ground. Then they started with two simple one-man suborbital flights, then a short orbital flight, then more incremental steps until the successful moon landing. That's what we're doing."

"Yes, but even during the moon program there was a catastrophic fire that caused an eighteen-month setback, not to mention the near-death experience of Apollo 13. As far as I can tell, even if Alan Shepard had crashed and gotten crushed to death it wasn't the end of the world. This could be."

"Don't worry. I have absolute faith in this program and you should, too."

"But what if some small thing I say or do, something that seems totally inconsequential, sets off a chain of events that alters the entire course of history," Eryk questioned.

"By the time your training is finished you'll be dreaming in flickering black and white like a nickelodeon, and you'll try to jump in a buggy to go to the general store. Your thoughts and words will be automatic.

"Besides, we have contingency plans. For one, we might send you back to repair what you screwed up, if you don't die on us. In any case, we are prepared to move the machine to a totally isolated, safe place with a specially selected crew. The crew is a cross-section, all from different geographic areas and lineages around the world, so if history is altered at least some of them will remain. If something happens and, God forbid, I should suddenly cease to exist, one of *them* will go back to repair the damage. I certainly have no intention to cut my own life off prematurely."

Trice didn't want to say that another one of the contingency plans also involved Eryk but in a more personal way. If Eryk screwed it up and they had to, they would go back and kill him as an infant. That way, if he was never born or died young, he would never have gone back in time. Whatever damage he caused would be eradicated by his non-existence. If Eryk changed history in a way they didn't like, Trice felt that he was unavoidably expendable.

"You will be thoroughly briefed," Trice continued. "You will know exactly what to do and how to act. Every scrap of information we can get our hands on about the time and place you are catapulted into will be drummed into your head until you believe you lived it yourself."

"That means you know where I am going and who I'll be?"

"Yes, with Heller's assistance. We've scoured diaries and journals from our target time frame a hundred to a hundred and twenty years ago. That's one of the historic periods we're targeting, the one that's farthest back.

"We've found the perfect identity for you to assume. It suits your background and our needs, and it's for a man with few connections anyone can trace. He kept a journal of sorts for two months and then apparently discarded it. A young woman he met found it and saved it, really treasured it. According to some of her letters, she expected to hear from the man again, but she never did. He's a man with almost no footprint. We can't find any trace of him anywhere after that. He may have died an obscure, forgotten death shortly thereafter. That's important because if we decide to send you back there again, you can operate anonymously."

"That sounds too cloak-and-dagger to me. Who is this person? Who will I become?"

"Your name will be 'Ian Larkin'. You were born on January 16, 1883. Your father was a Welch immigrant who settled in Henderson, Kentucky where he worked in the coal mines. Your mother died in childbirth when you were six after two prior miscarriages. Instead of having a younger sibling, you were an only child."

"But I'm Polish."

"Do you think you can practice an Americanized Welch accent with a southern drawl until it's second nature?"

"Bloody hell. What do you think of me?" Eryk's effort sounded more Irish than Welch.

"That's awful! I have a mind to send you back in time to see Henry Higgins first. For now, let me continue with what we know. A neighbor introduced you to the piano when you were young and you took to it right away, so much so that your father purchased a cheap D. F. Beatty upright for you for $105. He wanted you to have the benefits of an education. It sounds like you never worked in the coal mines as a child yourself, at least not during the school term. Maybe during the summers, we don't know. With no other family to support, your father probably made enough for the two of you to get by. You lived with your father at least until you were seventeen, then he died in a mining accident a year or two later.

"At around that time you obtained a scholarship to Cecilian College in Elizabethtown, Kentucky to study history, with high recommendations from your secondary school teachers and headmaster. After attending Cecilian for six years, you earned an A.M. degree. You also maintained your interest in piano, taking elective music classes from the music department when you could. Your other passion was baseball which you followed avidly.

Unfortunately, as far as we can tell, you weren't anywhere near good enough to make the Cecilian baseball team. You weren't on any team rosters we could find.

"After graduating, you continued tutoring at the school to save some money. You also sent letters and applications to schools where you hoped to secure a more permanent teaching position. Towards the end of this period, you started a sporadic journal. After six months you left the school to explore and interview at schools in five medium sized towns. Maybe you wanted to go somewhere that reminded you of Henderson where you grew up. Your first stop was for an interview at Lawrence College in Appleton, Wisconsin, for a position as an instructor in history and English.

"Unfortunately, we don't have records or copies of any papers or dissertations you wrote, no letters of introduction or applications you might have filled out, so we'll have to fake something. We'll also make you a copy of Larkin's journal using paper and ink authentic to the period. You will take that with you."

"Isn't that important? If there are any papers or letters of introduction, he could have been asked about them."

"We're still working on that. To continue, you first travelled to Chicago mostly by train, then arrived in Appleton by a Chicago and Northwestern Railway train on Wednesday September 4, 1907. You interviewed on October 1, and apparently left Appleton for St. Louis on October 15 when you failed to obtain the position in Appleton. That's when the journal stopped.

"We've been unable to find records of any other relatives except an aunt on your mother's side who lived in New York City, nor can we find any records for Ian Larkin from November 1907 onwards. There were probably relatives back in Wales, but we can't trace it."

"What's next?"

"For you, intensive training and preparation. I'm afraid you won't be home much before your exchange. I'll see to that." "Why?

Don't forget early twentieth century America is my specialty. I already have most of the background."

"By the time Heller and I are through you'll think you actually are Ian Larkin and you're actually visiting 1907 Appleton. As you know by now, I'm very thorough and I don't leave anything to chance.

"Heller has a full briefing for you with everything we know about life, politics, leading citizens, business, schools and their faculties and teachers, mining and technology, popular culture, current events, town news, local geography, street maps, transportation, and all the rest of it in Henderson and Elizabethtown, Kentucky. Don't read any Appleton newspapers including what's mentioned in the journals so you can have a fresh reaction when you get there.

"I want you to study up on baseball in the early 1900s. Memorize all the teams, their players, batting averages, won-lost records, all of the other statistics for the previous five or six years. You're a baseball freak anyway."

"I prefer the term 'expert'."

"Call yourself what you want. Just don't bet on any games while you're there."

"I think you'd better try to find out about Ian's childhood friends and figure out what they might have known about him if you can. Any kind of letters, diaries, recollections, anecdotes.

"I do think it's important to know if Ian ever worked in the mines. Maybe Ian Larkin is on a payroll list or in a small-town newspaper article in Henderson. That's information the schools, references, or other people Ian could have encountered might have. It would be in his application, and somebody might talk to references who would have that information. I'd also better know his subjects, teachers, grades, and school activities, and as much as possible about the faculty, names of other students, course offerings, school sponsored activities, things like that at both Henderson and Elizabethtown. Someone is likely to ask about it."

"We are trying to get that information and we have some of it, but most of it just doesn't seem to exist anymore. I have an intern still working on it, but I'm not optimistic he'll find out a lot more. Those kinds of records are hard to come by if they even still survive, and there's nobody around to ask. If there are any records are preserved anywhere, I guarantee you I'll find them."

"Please do everything you can. I don't want to blow my cover."

"Don't worry. We're going to rehearse every event in the journal. We are going to make up scenarios for anything that might happen to you and rehearse for those, too. We'll find a way to fake what we don't know.

"I'm going to discover every crack in your knowledge of the time. You have to know every nuance of what daily life was like, at least everything we know about. To make sure, I'm sending you on field trips. You're going to every location, train station and historically preserved outhouse. You'll visit working coal mines and get dirty yourself. You'll know about every local politician and big shot of the times in both towns. You'll read the local speeches you might have heard and the newspapers and magazines you might have read prior to September 4, 1907. You'll see every building and artifact that's been preserved along with every period photo we can find. You'll even eat the foods of the times."

"Hopefully not prepared by you."

"I take that as a challenge. What do you think of soda biscuit and hominy, or poor man's pudding, or maybe some panned hare? Consider yourself a guinea pig. Do you have any more questions?"

"Are you sure I can't be Polish? That's the second largest immigrant group in Wisconsin after German. There aren't that many Welch there."

"Then don't start a trend. Be historically accurate at all times. At least I can see that both of us worry about all of the details."

"What about staying healthy. There were no antibiotics and you won't force me to use nineteenth century snake oil."

"I've already thought about that. You are about to receive every vaccination known to man. We just hope modern strains are similar enough to the ones they had back then. We have supplements for you to take, and we plan to put you on a healthy diet and exercise program to build you up. You'll look like Harry Houdini himself before we're through with you."

"Please! Will you handcuff me to the time machine, too?"

"Ian Larkin bought tickets to St. Louis on October 11, after his rejection by the Lawrence that day, departing on the 15th. His journal stops on the 13th. We'll do the reverse exchange that evening while Ian is in his hotel room. Remember, you have to come back from Appleton with exactly the things we are sending you with, no more and no less. You have to leave anything you buy or receive there, and bring back everything you went with.

"Maybe Mr. Larkin planned to take an inner-city from St. Louis to his next school, McKendree College in Lebanon, Illinois. We don't need to worry about that as long as he finds the tickets in his room when we return him."

"What about the journal? Do I leave it for someone to find or bring it back? And where would I leave it?"

"That's a damn good question. We know what room and boarding house Larkin stayed in, so leave it there if you don't find it. If he has it on him when we grab him, we'll keep it. I should think he would keep the journal on him or in his bags."

"What if he doesn't? Besides, the handwriting won't exactly match. I think I'd better come back with it. These sorts of small things could have big repercussions. It's a big risk."

"I'll have to think about that. Keep your eyes and ears open, see what you can find out when you're there. I don't want you to have to freelance it."

* * *

"What did you come up with?" Eryk asked.

Heller tasked Watkins with putting Eryk/Ian's wardrobe together. They all decided he could get by with two suitcases, an umbrella, and a fairly cheap gold-plated pocket watch.

"I have a list," Sandy answered. "The hard part was to make everything authentic. We don't want anything to look off and arouse the least suspicion. Duplicating the fabrics, umbrella, and personal use items, knowing the exact makeup of the materials, and exactly duplicating the same level of craftsmanship when the craftsmen are long dead isn't so simple. We used museum samples and antiques we found and tried to compensate for the deterioration."

"The most important thing to me is to get the clothing right. I gave you a list of what *I* thought I needed."

"Well, first off, I have a straight razor for you."

"For heaven's sake, I thought you said authenticity was the hard part. Like cutting my own throat is nothing."

"Relax, you'll get lots of practice first. If your head stays on, you'll be ready, otherwise I'm recommending Heller to take your place so she can't annoy me anymore."

The two of them were in a small conference room with a table strewn with antique magazines and clothing samples cobbled up by the prop department. Watkins kept examining and fidgeting with some of the jackets and shirts. At least he wasn't playing with the straight razor.

"You'll have three shirts with detachable cuffs and collars, cufflinks and pearl studs, a pair of sleeve garters, five pairs of socks with garters and underwear, the straight razor with a folding wood handle and a leather strop, a soft brush and cup, aftershave and cologne, a pair of pleated and cuffed slacks with a matching jacket, a comb, hair slick, two bars of lye soap, a small mirror, some pencils, and fifteen sheets of writing paper," Watkins continued. "You don't smoke, drink, or chew tobacco so you don't need any of the paraphernalia that goes with that."

"Do you have the wardrobe I requested to wear during the transition? I want a dark blue three-piece serge suit with peg top cuffed pants, high buttons, and high narrow lapels; a blue silk tie; a tall silk hat; a walking stick with a silver-plated handle; a gold-plated watch and fob; leather gloves; comfortable leather shoes; and a decent top coat with minor wear. I want a tailored fit but not too tight, and I want everything to show some very slight wear."

"It's in the works. You should grow your hair out longer. Before you leave a hair stylist will part it in the middle or a bit left of center, cut and style it the way it was done in 1907, and slick it down." "That's also in the works. I'm growing it as we speak." Just then Heller walked in.

"What's all this?" She turned to Watkins. "Why are you bothering to pick out clothes for him? He only wears what his wife tells him to." Turning to Eryk she said, "Isn't that right?" "I'm not amused," Eryk responded.

"Let's be realistic. The entire time you're gone you'll be wondering what your wife is up to. Do you want me to spell it out for you? She won't have *you* on her mind. Now what are you going to do about it? You'd better do something now before it's too late."

* * *

Trice was a humorless but thoughtful and by no means unpleasant man. Every once in a great while he would get animated about some topic that excited him and erupt out of his normal mechanical manner in an interesting way.

He seemed to be a dependable straight shooter.

According to everyone, he had a marked technical bent bordering on genius. Eryk was convinced that in some past life, in another century, Trice was a wildly successful watchmaker in a small European country. Everything was in its precise place and work was systematic and methodical. Each step in every process was carefully monitored and evaluated, then his forward strategy was adjusted.

"Eryk, just imagine how it could be if the world ran smoothly and everyone played their role and followed the rules to the letter?" Trice said. "Imagine if there were no malevolent sociopaths to throw banana peels on everyone's sidewalk. No selfish rogue despots, no larcenous criminals or monopolists, no con men or self-important dictators that prey on everyone else. Get some charismatic demagogue or fanatic in front of a crowd and he will lead them astray every time, especially if there's a grievance. People will follow him enthusiastically while he sets the trap. After all, people are herd animals because they're social and they are ripe for an enticing pitch.

"It doesn't have to be that way. Society could be a well-oiled machine without these people to jam up the gears. You can help change all that. How can you refuse to help? Wouldn't it be immoral not to?"

"True," Eryk thought to himself. He sat up straight in his chair, not wishing to be the only thing out of place in Trice's office. "There's no unemployment in an ant colony. This is just the kind of sentiment I expect from Trice." It was one of Trice's rare animated outings. What Eryk actually said was, "Maybe, but there has never been a utopia."

"The far-sighted geniuses, the ones who find medical cures and create labor saving tools to ease the cares of everyday life, those are the ones who should be encouraged. Poverty, hunger, unemployment, and many forms of abuse would be minimal. Work on diseases and public infrastructure would progress rapidly. Everyone's life would be so much better."

"Nobody can disagree with that."

"So now," Trice continued, "what if Lenin, Vlad III, Ho Chi Min, Yakubu Gowon, Nicholas II, Leopold II, and all the other murderous dictators never existed? What if Archduke Ferdinand was never assassinated and World War I never started? Without World I there would have been no German reparations or hyperinflation, and the environment that allowed Hitler to rise wouldn't have existed. The Holocaust and loss of life and the terrible destruction of Europe in World War II would never have come about. Without World War I the unpayable indebtedness a lot of nations incurred to fight the war, and the subsequent spiral of debt that built up after the war wouldn't have gotten underway. When the metastasizing pile of debt finally collapsed it brought about the Great Depression; probably that could have been avoided. Do you see what I mean?"

Eryk knew better than to disagree with Trice's spirited logic. He recalled that the roots of World War I were a lot more complex and prolonged, and actually lay in ethnic strife in the Balkans, governments that trampled ethnic sensibilities, and a buildup of local tensions and wars. The assassination was just the flashpoint.

Eryk objected, "You pointed out yourself that if you change history, millions of people who are alive now will never be born, and others who don't exist now will take their place. We might not be around anymore ourselves. Would you play God that way?"

"That's why I need talented historians like you. The changes have to be made surgically, very carefully. If there *are* any mistakes, we need the ability to go back and correct it. I have a plan in my head and it will work."

"And who is on your assassination list?"

"There will be no assassinations because there are humane alternatives. People's lives can be steered in different directions. They can be relocated to different circumstances, kidnapped if necessary. Their mothers can marry different men."

"A lot depends on the times," Eryk reminded Trice. "What would Houdini be without Vaudeville? What if Hitler was in the Roman Senate instead of Germany? What if Napoleon had been a figure on the American frontier? I find it difficult to predict the outcome of this experiment."

"I'm taking that into account."

When Trice had left Watkins turned to Eryk. "You know, if you go through with this, a time will come when you have to make a choice: pursue your own happiness and quest for history or give them up so this current generation can live. You know that don't you?"

"That's down the road. I'm hoping that when the time comes, I can find alternatives so I won't be trapped like that."

"It won't be up to you. History is broader than you are."

* * *

The big moment had arrived.

Eryk went to the transfer compartment to await the countdown.

Sandy and Heller were already there.

"Where's Trice?" Eryk asked. "This is the beginning of his big moment."

"He said he'd be delayed and we should go ahead without him if we have to. He had an important phone call. The machine is already sequencing so you better get in tight now," Heller replied.

A mechanical voice wailed "Twenty seconds…" Eryk positioned himself inside the cramped stainless-steel box, a finely dressed sardine with a suitcase in each hand.

The voice continued, "Ten, nine, eight…" The door automatically started to close and seal itself.

Meanwhile, Trice was finishing his call. "It's all set Natalie. Eryk will be out of town for just over six weeks and he can't come back until he's finished his assignments. (Pause) "Just trust me. The project is classified and I'm not at liberty to divulge the details. I rented a hotel room for the entire six weeks. I'll send you a text messages to tell you when to be there. Pay attention and follow the schedule I give you exactly. Please don't disappoint me. You know I can't stand it when people don't follow their instructions." (Pause) "Don't concern yourself with it. I'll take care of my wife. I know how to handle her. I've planned a series of family emergencies for her to deal with."

Chapter Five
Secrets

Eryk suddenly found himself standing on a wooden train platform with his two worn suitcases. It was chilly with occasional light rain, maybe in the low sixties but Eryk barely noticed. He was transfixed, the unfamiliar scene trying to register in his mind. He was in a movie set but it was real he told himself. The damp chill didn't penetrate his coat. The drops materialized unrecognized on his shoulders. A large clock on the gable of the wooden building said it was 11:23 in the morning.

He looked around. There were men in suits with pocket watches, men in working clothes with open collar shirts, many with suspenders, a few with vests, all pounding out the thud-thud noise of shoe leather on wooden planks as they scurried about. There were women in long cotton dresses and others in long skirts and shirtwaists. Nobody talked to a cellphone or had a Bluetooth in their ear.

Eryk felt suddenly out of place and alone. It was totally surreal. Training and practice were one thing, but he didn't fit in. He was completely out of sync and out of touch. How could he pass himself off as a man of the times if everything was foreign? What an inauspicious start!

Eryk was the Guinea pig, the world's first time traveler. The machine had only been tested by sending objects to the future, to rematerialize at a pre-calculated day and time. Would it work correctly in the other direction? The times looked real but was this the Appleton station? There had to be a sign on either side of the building facing the direction of the tracks that announced the name of the station. What was the day and year?

Eryk/Ian stepped inside the station, out of the rain. There was a ticket window, an office, a newsstand, a telegraph office, a schedule board, and four rows of benches. He shuffled across the wooden floor to the newsstand. "Do you have an Evening Crescent or a Daily Post?"

"Both, yesterday's. Today's ain't in. Which do ya want?"

"One of each."

"That's two cents apiece. Where ya from? Strange accent. Are ya foreign?"

"Born in Kentucky, father Welch."

"Whatcha doin' in Appleton? Ain't no mines 'round here."

"Looking for a job at Lawrence."

"No mines there either, I'm afraid."

"They have an opening for an instructor position."

"Better learn your English first so ya don't sound so funny."

"Thanks, I'll work on it."

Eryk/Ian decided he had better keep his mouth shut and just eavesdrop on the people in the station to find out what was in the air. His southern Welch-English was obviously a bit off.

He glanced at the papers before stuffing them in a suitcase. The papers were dated September 3, 1907. It looked like Trice's calculations were right on the money. He was, unfortunately, two days late to hear the Labor Day speeches where he could have found out who the important town personages were and what was on people's minds. Maybe he would find some accounts in the papers.

Eryk prepared himself to step into his 1907 persona. This was what he wanted, to experience what it was really like to live in another time, to be immersed in all the details and minutiae that had been lost to historians over the years. Different concerns, different routine, no computers, fewer conveniences, and no Natalie or Dr. Trice; they were more than a century in the future. Eryk settled in and started to feel free, like a new, single man with a southern pedigree and a twentieth century future.

Eryk, that is Ian, decided not to hoof the five blocks down

Appleton Street to Lawrence Street in the rain. Instead, he took the Oneida Street trolley to Lawrence Street, then walked east a couple of blocks to what was then numbered 768, Mrs. Lizzie Bowe's Boarding House near Morrison Street, the house where Ian stayed. From the platform he ambled down some steps, dodged the horse-cabs, and reminded himself to pay attention to where he stepped.

Eryk/Ian rang the bell and a woman answered. "I'm Ian Larkin. Do you have any rooms available? I need a place for the next six weeks, maybe longer. I'll pay cash up front."

"I'm Lizzie Bowe, owner o' dis house." Eryk saw a fiftyish Irish woman with a care-worn but pleasant face. "Two Lawrence students occupy one of da rooms and t'ere's a couple in another, but I have space on the second floor. What kind of board ya looking for?"

She had a room costing $4.50 a week half-board, available for the six weeks, rather high but Eryk took it anyway considering its proximity to the school. It came with a wash bowl and a pitcher. More importantly, it was Ian's room that was available. It faced south, warm, spacious enough, near the shared hall bathroom, well-furnished and comfortable. The Park Hotel would have been nicer and right across from Lawrence College, but Ian didn't stay there. There was a piano in the parlor and Eryk/Ian knew he would have to try it out later.

"Dinner's in half an hour at twelve thirty," Mrs. Bowe stated. "Will ya be joinin' us?"

"I'm looking forward to it," Eryk/Ian responded.

In the late nineteenth and early twentieth centuries boarding houses were common, although hotels and rooming houses started to replace them after 1900. They were a dependable source of income for the owner. They were usually family homes in which rooms were rented out for extra income. They might be owned by a mature single woman or widow, or by a couple whose children had grown up and moved out. The woman of the house normally ran the boarding operation while the husband, if there was one, worked elsewhere.

Lodgers might stay for a few days or a few years.

The parlor and dining room were shared by everyone in the house; usually the limited number of bathrooms were also shared. Rent generally included one to three meals each day. Boarders typically had a choice of bed-and-breakfast, half-board (bed, breakfast, and dinner), or full-board (bed, breakfast, dinner, and supper). Dinner was the biggest meal of the day eaten at midday or in the early or late afternoon. Supper was a smaller evening or late evening meal. Owners and guests ate their meals together.

Boarding houses had strict rules the guests were expected to adhere to. For example, guests might be allowed only one hot bath a week (cold baths anytime). In a few of them guests were not allowed in the house during daylight hours, although this was not a typical rule.

Eryk/Ian freshened up in his room, picked out a few newspapers articles to read and went downstairs to eat. He was joined by two twentyish male students, a young ordinary-looking couple maybe in their mid-twenties, and after she brought the food, Mrs. Bowe. The students wore dress pants with suspenders and opencollared dress shirts, the woman wore a blue frilly blouse and long dress, and the man wore a grey suit. Eryk/Ian confined his conversation to the weather and yesterday's newspaper contents.

Dinner consisted of boiled beef with potatoes, turnips, corn, pickled beets, apple pie, white cake with walnuts, and coffee, a very acceptable meal.

By all rights, after dinner Eryk/Ian should rest up after his long and arduous train trip, but since his travels were over in an instant and his short walk from the trolley stop didn't amount to much, he grabbed his umbrella, and went out to explore the street.

It was a block north to College Avenue where there was another trolley and numerous commercial establishments. Eryk/Ian concentrated on the two blocks of College Avenue directly north of

the boarding house. His first stop was the Union News Depot a block
to the west, just past Saecker and Rogers Furniture and Undertaking
and the Chicago Record-Herald office.

"Do you have today's Crescent and Post?" he asked the
proprietor.

"Daily Post."

"I'll take it," Ian replied.

"Any particular story interest ya?" the proprietor asked.

"Baseball news. I want to read about all the scores and all the
angles." Eryk/Ian figured baseball was a good neutral subject. He
could talk about it at length and not slip up and reveal himself.

"Looks to me like the Cubs are a sure t'ing in the National
League, 'n so?"

"I don't see anybody who can catch 'em."

"Who ya like in the American League'?"

"Detroit and Philadelphia both look like winners. I think the
Sox will fade in the stretch."

"The Sox are close. I t'ink day make a run for it but my
money's on Philly ya know."

Eryk/Ian knew otherwise but he held his tongue. "Sounds like
a good bet to me."

Eryk/Ian gave the proprietor two cents for the paper and
automatically started to add in another penny for the sales tax. Then he
realized, no sales tax! Every price and wage was exactly what it said,
no more and no less.

He tucked the paper under his arm and continued on to his next
destination at the west end of the block, Pearson's Music House. He
could have used a plastic bag to protect his newspaper, but plastic was
just now being invented. He had to settle for tucking it under his arm,
protected from the intermittent drizzle beneath his umbrella.

College Avenue was a broad ninety-six foot wide picturesque
and comfortable street with parallel trolley tracks running down the

middle of most of it. Sidewalks were a wide sixteen feet. Plenty of pedestrians went about their business. They competed with a smattering of horses and horse carriages, bicycles, and automobiles, all dodging pedestrians and the frequent enough streetcars.

There are more than a few small towns and historic districts in every state with buildings reminiscent of the late nineteenth and early twentieth century, and this street reminded Eryk of some of them he had seen, in Thurmond, Harper's Ferry, and Charles Town, West Virginia among others. Appleton had an eclectic architectural mix of American Renaissance, Art Nouveau, Chicago school, modernisme, and other architectures. Most of the buildings were two- or three-story brick. Many of the buildings on the north side had large awnings extending out over the sidewalk.

There were no walls of glass and steel here. There were no concrete monoliths adorned with tall windows and steel-railed balconies, and with a bit of stone or glass façade thrown in, pretending to be something they weren't. Every building had its own variation in style. Every building was genuine with a distinct personality worn on its own sleeve.

There was a charming juxtaposition of the old and the new, cars, horses and pedestrians all at seeming cross-purposes; the smell of car fumes mixed with horse droppings; the sound of honking horns interspersed with horses naying. It imparted a strong sense of motion, a confused vector pointing from old to new, an impending sense of purpose and progress thrust upon everyone there. You never got that feeling from 21st century architecture.

Along the way to Pearson's, Eryk/Ian passed Schlafer Hardware which rented bicycles, and on the opposite side the Fox River Valley Telephone Company where he could make phone calls, as well as the Wisconsin Telephone Company where he could also make phone calls.

Pearson's sold music and a line of music-related goods, but they specialized in selling pianos and organs. Eryk/Ian picked up a few pieces of sheet music and a large paper bag to protect them while explaining to a persistent salesman he couldn't afford a new piano to play them on at the moment.

Crossing over to the other side of the street and heading back to the boarding house, Eryk/Ian's next exploration took him to Matt Schmidt Hatter and Men's Furnisher. Eryk stopped to take a look at the new "American" fashions. Prices were high and the store was busy despite the weather. They featured suits with jackets and vests, pleated pants with suspenders or a belt, ties, and collared shirts. The jackets tended to have three or four buttons and high, narrow lapels.

A good hat typically cost one to three dollars; a suit might run anywhere from ten to thirty dollars, for example, a Hart Schaffer and Marx suit was between 18 and 25 dollars; a top coat could run between ten and twenty-five dollars, while a good pair of leather shoes were four or five dollars. Prices were dropping on account of improved manufacturing and mass production, but clothing still put a sizable dent in the lower-class budget.

"Anything on sale?" he asked a clerk.

"Work wear. What do ya do?"

"Looking for a teaching position."

"Our suits, vests, and ties aren't on sale, but you should consider a new suit for yourself. People will notice if ya look the part, ya know."

"I'm not sure I can afford your prices right now," Eryk/Ian said in an attempt to haggle.

"Den why don't ya try back during the school year. We have denims if ya need any." Public schools were back in session on Monday the 9th while the fall semester at Lawrence would start on the eleventh.

It was a similar story at Woehler and Healy and at Joseph Spitz, which specialized more in women's attire. Women's shirtwaists, that is, blouses, were in style combined with a long skirt. Frills, lace, and bows were standard and the more the better. Middle and especially upper-class women almost always wore corsets. Both men and women usually wore hats, which, in a status-conscious age, transformed from small to huge and gaudy over time. In fact, the plumage on women's hats became so elaborate that some bird species experienced a population crash. By 1907, Wisconsin had passed a law that bird feathers and bird parts were forbidden in clothing.

Fashion was becoming Americanized and was no longer necessarily derived from Victorian and European styles. In consequence, American dress was ridiculed by European observers.

Styles were evolving from the practical to a more ornamental style, and clothing was very much becoming an expression of class, aspirational if not actual. Comfort was less important than conveying one's high status to others, or quite often, the class one wished to belong to. Quality of fabric might be a giveaway. A good new suit might indeed make a difference at Ian's interview.

Store fronts, magazines, and mail-order catalogs made it clear to everybody what the latest fashions were.

Since dress codes tended to be formal, some would say too formal, there was too much façade and pretention hiding the genuine article. Common workplace dress, for example, for factory and office workers, tended towards utilitarian formality. Middle- and upper-class families dressed formally for dinner, even if they were not having company. Upper-class gentlemen changed their clothes three or four times a day and made sure they were suitably dressed for each of the day's events. Although formality and ostentation held sway especially among the upper classes, to Eryk, people's appearance was refreshing, and you can't fault anyone for trying to look their Sunday best regardless of the outcome.

It was still a damp, cool and rather dreary day. Eryk had just a few more stops to make, all within two blocks of the boarding house, before getting a bite to eat and settling in for the evening.

He took a quick glance around in "My Store, J C Ferber, proprietor," a general merchandise store, before heading for Wollman's Bazaar four doors away to browse a few of the books and magazines. He planned to return in a few days for a thorough investigation.

Two doors further down past the Appleton Crescent office was the Appleton Music Company with a large selection of sheet music. Eryk/Ian bought "To a Wild Rose" by Macdowell, "In the Shade of the Old Apple Tree" by Williams and Alstyne, "Toyland" by Victor Herbert, and five Joplin pieces, "Maple Leaf Rag", "The Entertainer", "The Cascades", "The Nonpareil" and "Heliotrope Bouquet," all for a quarter. The price of sheet music had dropped drastically due to better printing methods, and was now quite affordable.

Griffin's Restaurant was a block back towards the boarding house. The real Ian had eaten there. Maybe they had Kentucky Fried Chicken.

On arriving at Griffin's Restaurant, Eryk seated himself in a corner away from the window. A waitress in a long black skirt and a frilly white blouse brought him a menu.

"Haven't seen ya here before. Live around here?"

"Hope to," the newly christened Ian replied. "I'll be interviewing at Lawrence. Hope to be an instructor there."

"What a strange accent you're havin'. Don't sound the least German. Where ya from?"

"Born and raised in Kentucky. My father was a Welch coal miner but he came here to find work."

"My name is Karen. I hope ya plan on bein' a regular here," she said with a half wink. "Best food in town, ya know. Just ask Maggie Griffin herself."

"I'm counting on it," he smiled back. "I'm Ian, Ian Larkin." He noticed a turkey dinner on the menu for twenty cents. "Can you recommend the turkey dinner?"

"One o' Maggie's specialties. What can I get ya ta drink?"

Good grief, what would Ian have drunk? Coffee might be a safe order, but how would he take it, black, sugar and cream? Or maybe his Welch father taught him to drink tea. These kinds of details could prove fatal. "Bring me water for now, then I'll have whatever desert you recommend."

"Comin' right up." Karen turned and headed for the kitchen.

Eryk/Ian opened up the day's Post and started to devour it. If Karen glanced his way again, he didn't notice. When he was finished, before he left the restaurant, he wanted to leave Karen a generous tip, an inducement for future good service and good will in case he slipped and said something he shouldn't and had to ask her to keep a secret for him. He left 15 cents.

The final destination was three doors past the Appleton Crescent office, Schell Brothers Grocers.

He bought some fresh fruits and vegetables, crackers, and jerky, things he could eat that the next morning and evening. He was leaving too early for breakfast at the boarding house. He waited for the clerk to ask him "paper or plastic", but instead he just put it all in a paper bag.

Shopping spree over, Eryk/Ian headed back to his room to read his newspapers, eat a late snack, wait for the next morning, and most important of all, stay out of trouble.

But that evening he couldn't resist slipping back to the parlor to pound out his rendition of Joplin's "The Nonpareil" to the delight of the other boarders.

* * *

Thursday September 5th dawned clear and dry with temperatures in the low 70s, a perfect fall day. It would have been a monumental waste to let such a beautiful day slip away, and it happened that Ian's journal called for a trip to Green Bay to see the Al G. Barnes Circus, so off Eryk went bright and early at 7 o'clock. The real Ian probably never saw a circus before this, or at least not a big one, in Henderson. In an age of internet, movies, TV, and a thousand other diversions Eryk never got excited about the circus. Sure, he had gone to a circus once as a teen, in a large indoor arena, but it just seemed like a lot of acrobatics, not like the slick staged tricks you see all the time in the media. However, this was a full-blown circus set in its time, with all the side shows, raw sights and smells, barkers, and charm that modern streamlined, sanitized, and slickly promoted circuses lack.

By 1900 there were dozens of circuses crisscrossing the country. Wisconsin was a prolific birthing center for them, some originating before 1850. The big two circuses, Ringling Brothers and Barnum and Bailey both had roots there. In 1907 unsubstantiated rumors circulated that Ringling Brothers was buying out Barnum and Bailey. The later had visited Appleton August 2nd, but the smaller but still substantial upstart Al G. Barnes Circus was unique in its own way.

The Barnes Circus originated in 1895 as a single act, but grew at an astounding pace and was quite large by 1907. It carved out its own niche specializing in wild animal acts.

Every respectable circus entered town in grand fashion, parading down the main street after disembarking from their railroad flatcars.

Circus parades could be anywhere from a block long to a mile long. They were spectacular affairs, and never failed to generate bountiful ticket sales from the overawed crowd that gathered to watch. It might begin with large elephants or other animals and a steam calliope, followed by colorful gaudily decorated wagons carved out with dragons and all manner of beasts, red-plumed horses decked out like part of a Roman army, decorated wagons with caged smaller animals, possibly floats and carriages with carved beasts or other themes for larger circuses, elephants with their necks graced by beautifully costumed performers, hordes of other large wild animals, parading acrobats and jugglers, costumed Greek gods and mermaids and other characters, clowns and harlequins hamming it up, wagonloads of freaks, and a large fancy six or eight horse wagon with the circus's combined bands blaring away. It was a grand spectacle indeed thundering down the dusty road. The smell of the animals lingered well after the parade itself, stimulating still more customers to come forward.

The Barnes half-mile parade of the time was always headed by Al Barnes himself riding a mammoth elephant. The remaining stomping, bellowing wild animals that seemed to be barely under control threatened to overrun the town at any moment, ready to wreak havoc. Any relationship to a much tamer Macy's parade would be strictly imaginary. You don't see that kind of a mobile exhibition any more.

The parade would proceed to the rented field where the tents were set up and everything was readied for the next day's performances in a frenzy of well-choreographed evening and overnight activity. Management made sure the smell of animals and animal waste, sawdust, peanuts and popcorn, and a full catalog of other odors permeated the community, putting the block-wide smell from the typical 21st century barbeque pit to shame.

The Barnes Circus parade through Green Bay was on September 1st and Eryk was sorry he had to miss it. The first shows were on September 2nd.

Eryk, that is, Ian, bought his railway tickets Thursday morning. The plan was to arrive well before the first show, to watch the final setting up. He would wear his informal clothes and groom himself carelessly on purpose so as not to look well off. He hid most of his money in his secret pockets. Circuses of the time were a great place to get ripped off.

Eryk/Ian decided the easiest way was to take a horse cab from the Green Bay train station. Even before he first glimpsed the huge, white multi-pointed main tent, he was greeted by the aroma of hay and elephant droppings. At the circus entrance a barker extoled the mandevouring wild beasts ("We've only lost a few of our customers"), the "incredible aerial sensations with unbelievable acts of daring and bravery" and the "freaks of nature you have to see to believe." Eryk/Ian went to one of the entry ticket booths.

Ticket-masters, or ticket-mistresses since many circuses used pretty women to distract the men customers, sat in a high booth so they always looked down on the customers who had to reach up to head level to hand over the entrance fee of fifty cents. The ticket master had two important jobs: the first was to short-change customers who needed change. For this reason, Eryk brought exact amounts. The second job was to look down into the customer's wallet to see how much money he had. If the wallet had more than a few dollars, the ticket-master gave a nod to an employee disguised as a member of the crowd. The employee's job was to put a chalk mark on the back of the customer's coat. The chalk mark told other circus employees this customer had money and it was their duty to extract as much of it as they could in fees to see special acts. This is the origin of the term "mark."

The saying was "fifty cents to get in, five dollars to get out." Once inside the circus customers could see the big acts in the main tent that took place in from one up to seven separate 30-foot rings. However, side show acts, freaks of the freak shows, vaudeville acts, adults-only tents, other special attractions, and just plain scams were typically an extra charge each, often a nickel a head. The performers for these acts were paid a percentage of the gate, and the most popular acts made a pretty penny.

Just in case any customers had any money left, there was food for sale, including peanuts and popcorn, cotton candy, corn dogs, fried meat, sugary confections, and beer. Occasionally, if it wasn't a dry county or state, if it didn't offend local ordinance or religious sensibilities or customs, and depending on the day of the week, there might even be hard liquor for sale. Eryk/Ian came with his supply of nickels.

By now the smell of popcorn and roasted peanuts mixed with the other odors and became overpowering. Children ran around everywhere, some uncontrolled and underfoot. The crowd was packing close together. If you were near the entrance you were forced to move along with the herd. There was no other choice. You were pushed along to the ticket booths and the main tent.

Excited chatter, giggling kids, eyes and feet focused on one of the entrances to the big tent, the excitement was building. You couldn't help but be caught up in it. It didn't matter that it was all a well-choreographed art form by now, the mood was becoming hypnotic all the same. This was grand entertainment on a large scale, one of the spectacles of a lifetime for those assembled faces eagerly anticipating the buildup and start of the show.

Ticket holders were herded into the main tent and, more importantly, herded back out again to the money-making side shows after the main acts were over.

The ring master paraded into the big tent with the three opening acts, to the band playing Fucik's "Entry of the Gladiators," the march that was standard and expected then as now. Scantily clad men and women in Romanesque outfits standing on bareback rode around the three rings twice, followed by monkeys riding their ponies, followed again by packs of performing dogs, and trailed by clowns shoving and squirting one another totally out of formation. Some of the men and women jumped off the horses as they passed the middle ring for the second time and started climbing the ladders to the high wire while the horses trotted out the side entrance as they were trained to do. The dogs and clowns headed for the left ring, the monkeys on their ponies for the right. The ringmaster announced each of the acts. The show was on!

The crowd focused in. Everything was new and exciting. The world outside the tent vanished as if it never existed. Families sat together in the stands. Everyone clapped and cheered. The faces smiled or frowned but not a one was neutral.

The animals got larger and less tame as the show progressed. Successive acts brought out trapeze artists performing from the top of the tent with no safety net, acrobats and jugglers vaulting on and off each other's' shoulders, hyenas, performing brown and black bears, polar bears, trained seals, zebras, hippos, ostriches, and camels. Clowns performed their skits between acts.

The final set of acts brought out the huge performing elephants, a lion tamer, and a star of the show named Bert Nelson, "master of the most savage beasts" with his tigers, pumas, and leopards.

Eryk knew that four years hence, in 1911, Bert Nelson would be joined by 22-year-old Mabel Stark, billed as the world's first woman tiger trainer. Stark was a dead ringer for Mae West and in fact doubled for her in one of her films.

The audience was driven out of the main tent at once to face a gauntlet of side shows and food stands, and to make way for the next batch of "townies." On the way out Eryk/Ian quickly examined his jacket for chalk. Barkers enticed audiences into the side shows.

Some of the side show performers were permanent fixtures while others drifted in and out over time. Today there was a vaudeville tent with a drummer and pianist featuring singers, dancers, and musical performances. In other tents or sections of tents there was a sword swallower, a knife thrower, a magician, a fire eater, a "snake enchantress" accompanied by a three-piece band, an "oriental enchantress" also with a three-piece band, smoking monkeys, midgets performing with a seven-and-a-half-foot man, and a tattooed man and tattooed woman posing for the crowd. There was also a very popular strong man posing, demonstrating his strength, and challenging the audience to one-on-one or one-on-several wrestling contests. The latter was dangerous because it often led to a no-holds-barred free-forall fight between the townies and the "carnies." If any of the carnies were revealed as fakes, things could get ugly fast. Eryk/Ian gave wide berth to those kinds of acts.

At other performances there might be trained cockatoos or other birds, a rubber man or woman, a bear wrestler, a chariot act or race, smoking seals, deformed pets trained to perform comical feats, contortion acts, fortune tellers, or clairvoyants, but none of those today.

There was a mini-wild west show in one of the side tents with sharp shooting demonstrations, bareback riding, shoulder riding, a rough riding demonstration, and abbreviated jockey races. It had its own small band.

The gold of the circus was the natural-born freak shows, bearded ladies and children, Siamese twins, people missing arms or legs, misshapen midgets and other seriously deformed people, hermaphrodites, and "captured exotics." At first Eryk/Ian tried not to stare at the four-legged man or the pig-faced boy, after all, it's impolite. But everyone was staring intently. The performers wanted them to look. The more who did, the more money they made. Wasn't that the point?

Eryk/Ian went to the circus for an education. He didn't expect to really enjoy himself, but this was the art of showmanship at its finest. Everything was extreme, gaudy and completely over the top. You could only experience this kind of show in person. TV and the internet didn't do it justice. Well, maybe you could experience something similar at a movie theater with a four-story threedimensional screen, octophonic sound at 125 decibels, and scratch and sniff theater tickets.

Eryk/Ian hurried back to the train station after sampling most of the acts. He avoided the food in the interest of maintaining his health. He tried to keep in mind to think of himself as Ian. He was still rather detached and not sufficiently immersed in his role.

In his room that evening he read in The Crescent that there was a harvest dance at Mackville. Dancing was a wildly popular activity at the time. The musical "Comin' Through the Rye" was playing at the Appleton Theatre, tickets costing 15, 25, 35, and 50 cents. He noted with alarm a story that a corpse sat up in bed, scaring everyone else in the room to death. The living and the dead exchanged places that day.

When he went downstairs his piano selections for the evening were the "March Militaire" published in that day's Evening Crescent and Fucik's "Entrance of the Gladiators."

* * *

Friday the 6th was a carbon copy of Thursday. Eryk's tour of history would be brief and he wasn't about to waste such a fine day.

Since it was a workday Mrs. Bowe served breakfast promptly at 7:00. This consisted of apple slices, oatmeal, a slice of broiled ham, a poached egg, a slice of toast, and coffee.

Eryk/Ian's plan was to stop at the newsstand, two newspaper offices, and the bookstores along College Avenue to catch up on the past week's news and to pick up a typical sample of what people of the time were reading. After dinner he planned to go to a park to watch the people and study the books and magazines he bought, finally landing at Griffin's for supper at sunset.

He stopped first at the Union News Depot, then at the offices of the Chicago Record-Herald to see if they had any back issues of the Chicago paper he could buy (they didn't). Next came Wollman's Bazaar, which sold popular books and magazines, and finally he dropped in at the offices of the Appleton Crescent at the corner of College and Morrison, what was then numbered 758 College Avenue, a dusty, dingy, cramped basement office half submerged down some steps with its windows right at sidewalk level.

As Eryk/Ian glanced around, his gaze paused momentarily on a short young woman with black wiry hair and a flowered hat talking to a tall, somewhat gaunt man, a bit haggard and slightly hunched over. He recognized who she was. His immediate instinct was to go and talk to her since she would be a fountain of interesting stories and information, but he realized talking to *any* reporter was a dangerous move. He instantly withdrew his gaze.

It was too late.

The young woman caught his knowing glance at once. Her keen reporter's instincts took over and she stepped over to him.

"Do I know ya from somewhere?" she asked.

"No, we've never met," Eryk/Ian said truthfully in the most convincing tone of voice he could muster.

"He's lying," she thought to herself. She strongly suspected there was a story here somewhere. Here was a man with a strange accent, obviously from somewhere else, who nevertheless recognized her but wouldn't admit to it. It was clear to her he was hiding something of interest. As she was to write later, when someone is eager to talk their story is either self-serving or trivial. If they are reluctant to talk but seem to know something, they are probably hiding a tale you want to know and there is a worthwhile story to pursue. So, she thought, who is this man and why is he pretending he doesn't know me when his expression says otherwise?

"Ya looks familiar," she bluffed. "Where do I know ya from?"

"I can assure you we have never met." That much was true and Eryk/Ian hoped she would read it in his face.

"My name is Miss Edna Ferber. I don't remember seein' ya in Appleton before. Where are ya from?"

At only 22 Ferber was already a crack reporter. The Appleton Crescent hired her as a cub reporter right out of high school at the age of only seventeen. In a time when women reporters were assigned to write fashion and society columns, women's pages, advice for the lovelorn, and articles on the woman's viewpoint, Ferber was not only assigned hard news, she was encouraged to sniff out and track down worthy stories on her own. She did write a weekly society column every Saturday for a year and a half, but that was it. Then she was offered a position as a reporter for the Milwaukee Journal. She quickly honed her instincts, learning to read faces and gestures at a glance, to memorize her interviews without taking distracting notes, to take in scenes with one look, and all of the other skills a good reporter needs.

While living in a Milwaukee boarding house, Ferber returned home to Appleton by train every two or three weeks to be with her family (the fare was 25 cents each way coach, but she bribed the conductor to let her sit in first class).

"My name is Ian Larkin, from Kentucky. Arrived this past Wednesday. I'll be in town a month or so while I'm waiting to be interviewed for a position at Lawrence." Eryk/Ian hoped that would satisfy her. Better not volunteer any unnecessary information.

Ferber was dressed simply. Eryk had read that people considered her plain looking and sharp featured, but he found the 22year-old version attractive enough.

"Then I would like to welcome you to our community. This is my friend Mr. Byron Beveridge. He's a reporter here for the Crescent." She told herself, "Put him at ease; make him feel comfortable so he will talk freely, then see if he slips up."

"What kind of position will ya interview for?" she continued.

"They have an opening for an Instructor in History and English starting with the second semester that begins in February."

"I hope you will do Lawrence credit. Do you have experience to recommend ya?"

"I tutored for two years after graduation. I specialized in American history." This was turning into too much of an inquisition Eryk/Ian thought.

"Ya went to school in Kentucky, did ya?" she probed.

"Yes, Cecilian College."

"Well, good luck to you." She sensed she was becoming too inquisitive. Time to back off a bit. "Since you're new in town why don't ya let Mr. Beveridge show ya around when he has the time?" She exchanged a knowing glance with her former coworker. He realized she sensed there was a story here.

Thomas Byron Beveridge, who was 31 in 1907, was still single and living with his mother. Despite the modest size of the town (Appleton had a population of 16,000), he prided himself on being a reporter there and on his acquaintance with everyone worth knowing. He felt he had a keen nose for news, and whenever something significant happened he would ferret out the details. Beveridge's other interest was military. He was a lifelong member of the Wisconsin National Guard and had served as a lieutenant in the Spanish-American War, continuing to move up in rank after that brief war.

"Are you a reporter or an editor here yourself?" Eryk/Ian asked Ferber. He knew perfectly well she once was.

"I'm a reporter for the M'waukee Journal. Used to be a reporter here but they got a new city editor who's old fashioned and doesn't like women in the news room. Thinks we should all be home tending the house or teachin' school. So, I have to ask, do ya know anyone here in Appleton? Do ya know anyone who used to live here?"

"Not a soul. Lawrence sent a posting to other colleges that said they needed an instructor in history and English and a vocal instructor for the spring semester, so I applied."

"What do you think about our town? Interesting story, southern man from the coal mines goes nort' for a new life in academia. Interesting ring to it, don't ya think? If ya get the job Byron will write an article so everybody'll know who ya are. Wouldn't it be nice? You'll have plenty of friends."

"I'm sure a story about me would bore your readers to tears. I came a few weeks early to see if it's a town I'd like to live in."

"And what do you think?"

"Nice town. You have a lot of questions, don't you?"

"I'm sorry," she replied. "I suppose it's a habit of mine by now, being a reporter, ainna? Appleton isn't a nosy town like some but we do like to know who our visitors are, especially if they have friends or family here."

"I have a question for you. Do you have a connection with the J. C. Ferber store near the College? I stopped in there last Wednesday."

"Yes, it's my parents' store. I'm helping my sister with the store and takin' care of my father while my mother is away on business this weekend. I try to come back to Appleton every couplethree weeks. Why don't ya stop in? I have some influence there. I'll arrange a special discount just for you," she winked. "We treat our visitors well around here. We can chat some more. I have the inside scoop from when I worked for the Crescent. I'll fill ya in, whatever ya want to know."

"Sometime when I have the chance. You sell a lot of fancy hats in your store."

"My sister makes them. I think ya might have an interesting story to tell. Where's y'ur hometown? Is it also Kentucky? Is it a small town like this one?"

"I grew up in Henderson, Kentucky. It *is* a small town. I'm afraid you won't find anything interesting about me, though. What about you? Did you grow up here?"

"We moved around. Here, Kalamazoo, Michigan, Ottumwa, Iowa. What kind o' town is Henderson?"

"It's a mining town. My father was a miner. He moved there from Wales looking for work."

Ferber suddenly exploded. "Another Welch miner? Just what this town needs! Maybe you should move on!" She caught herself. "Excuse me. I had some bad experiences in a mining town full o' Welch miners. I'm not blaming you. So, you were born in Kentucky?"

"That's right."

He didn't seem Welch to her. She had been around plenty of Welch families in Ottumwa, but this man's accent was more northern and sounded like a trace of Irish, not Welch. His language was too sophisticated. His clothes weren't right, either. Too perfectly stitched and too symmetrical for a sweatshop seamstress. His gestures and his manner of speaking were just way too conservative.

"I still think y'u're familiar. Have ya ever been to Ottumwa or do ya have any relatives there?"

"No, my relatives are mostly back in Wales."

"Ever work the mines yourself?"

Here was a subject Eryk wanted to avoid at all costs because he didn't know the real answer. He had to finesse it, to have it both ways. "Yeah, a few months here and there. They put the boys to work picking the slate and debris from the coal as it slides down the chutes. It's dirty and dangerous and I'm not proud of it, so I don't like to talk about it. I've been telling people I didn't."

As Ferber later wrote, a reporter hones her techniques for extracting information from people who didn't want to spill it. They included being sympathetic and understanding, being insistent ("I won't leave here without a story"), browbeating ("I will get this story whether you cooperate or not; you may as well tell everyone your point of view if you want it represented"), playing on sympathy ("I'm just a girl cub reporter. If I go back without a story my editor will fire me. Won't you please help me out?"), the fake-out ("I already have the details; I just need you to corroborate"), or just turning on the charm, of which Edna Ferber possessed an overabundance.

One of her favorite techniques was to ask a leading question and just shut up. Don't say anything. Most people can't stand a silence and they will crack and say something, anything, and often what they say will be revealing. Car salesmen use this technique all the time. When their target finally speaks, they often say something like, "I prefer sporty red models," to which the salesman springs the trap and responds "I have exactly what you are looking for." She tried the first of her gambits.

"Why did ya stop at the Crescent? Do ya have a master plan?"

Eryk/Ian's unexpected counter-response was, "Is there anything here that would interest me?"

Not a small-town answer, turning it around with another question she thought. "I mean, is there anything we can help ya with?"

"I hoped to look through recent additions of the paper so I can learn more about Appleton and its people. I want to see if I would fit in. Do you have some recent editions?"

"Sure. Mr. Beveridge can assist ya with that since I don't work here anymore."

Beveridge finally had a chance to get a word in. Turning to Ferber he said, "Why not then? Y'u'll be going over to 'My Store' won't ya?"

Turning to Eryk/Ian, Beveridge continued, "Aren't you a historian? Care for some background, as we like to call it, about our town and about Wisconsin, right now?"

It was clear to both Ferber and Beveridge that no matter how dumb Eryk/Ian pretended to be, as the discussion progressed, it was obvious he was already familiar with most of their revelations. How on earth could this Ian Larkin know anything at all about their local history? It's not like a small-town library in Kentucky would have even a single article about some other small-town way up north. Both of them were more than a little suspicious. Had he already met someone from Wisconsin who filled him in, or was he hiding a secret?

Ferber asked, "Where ya stayin'? Byron can fetch you once the afternoon edition is out and show ya around, can't ya Byron?"

"I'm at the Bowe Boarding House but I prefer to explore on my own." What Eryk/Ian didn't want was to spend any more time with reporters.

"Why don't I just meet ya for supper then," Beveridge stated.

"How about the beginning of next week?" A weary Eryk/Ian threw in the towel.

"If ya need anything stop at 'My Store'. If I'm not there ask for Mrs. Julia Ferber. She'll be back Tuesday evening."

Ferber knew her mother was smart and observant. She would tell her to watch for Ian Larkin and talk to him, see what she could find out. Was this the real Ian Larkin she wondered? Was he an imposter? If so, what happened to the real Larkin? What was this man really doing and why? He was too smooth and sophisticated and his English was too polished to have spent an entire life in a small rural coal town.

Eryk/Ian, however, had no intention of ever setting foot in the store again, nor of finding a convenient afternoon to meet with Beveridge. Henceforth all research would be conducted at the public library. No more newspaper offices.

"I intend to write an article if ya get y'ur job. People here would find it interestin' what a visitor from a very different kind of small town thinks about their city, 'n so? Ya strike me as the observant kind, someone with insight, so why don't ya help me out?" Beveridge said.

"You overestimate me."

He was worried now. He never prepared for an encounter with Edna Ferber. What if this starts a chain of events that diverts her from her historical destiny? The course of many lives would also be altered. In the future she was destined to become a writer; she would win a Pulitzer Prize for her novel "So Big", she would write the novel "Showboat" which Jerome Kern and Oscar Hammerstein II turned into a musical, and she would write "Giant" which became a movie starring James Dean. What if pursuing this story helped keep her on the reporter track?

This was getting out of hand. He had to somehow force her and Beveridge back on track. He hoped he had satisfied their curiosity. They didn't understand the dangerous fire they were paying with.

At least, Eryk hadn't suddenly vanished into the ether. He seemed to still be in one piece after three days, but he sensed it was too good to last.

Chapter Six
Almost a Fine Week

Saturday was Eryk/Ian's time for a self-guided tour of the Lawrence campus. Registration for the upcoming semester was on Monday and Tuesday, while classes were starting on Wednesday, so now was the time to go before a lot of students started to arrive. The chilly rain that greeted him as he awoke wasn't going to stop a determined Eryk.

Neither Eryk nor the real Ian would want to look like an idiot, nor would they care to make the interviewer who invited him look stupid.

Most of the campus sat on a bluff three hundred feet above the north bank of Fox River. After walking around the campus, the first stop was the Main Hall which originally housed all of the administrative offices and classrooms. It was a four-story ivy-covered stone building with a classic architecture, having a grand portico in front and a large dome on top. Then there was the Sampson House, where college President Samuel Plantz, an ordained Methodist minister, lived. The Carnegie Library, a two-story gray brick and sandstone, was not currently open to students or visitors. Ormsby Hall, a dormitory for women, was one of the newest buildings. It featured indoor plumbing and a pleasing three-story architecture. The Stephenson Hall of Science was a well-equipped four-story gray brick and sandstone English classical style building. Unfortunately, Eryk/Ian found that its museum was closed.

The classrooms were open in the two-story portion of the observatory building where astronomy and mathematics were taught. The attached three-story dome capped observatory itself was closed to the public except on Wednesday evenings. It contained a ten-inch telescope, a spectroscope, and other equipment.

The Alexander gymnasium was open for use by Lawrence students and faculty, with a physical fitness instructor on duty. However, the Lawrence athletic field was located off-campus along the interurban trolley line to Kaukauna.

Finally, the original conservatory building was open and Eryk wandered in to look around. Classes were offered in voice, piano, organ, stringed instruments, and theory. Practice rooms were available for use by students and faculty. The building housed an organ and a number of first-class grand pianos which, of course, Eryk had to get his hands on. The pianos would certainly have been the best the real Ian had ever seen.

Eryk picked out "Honeysuckle Rose" to a slow, soft-shoe vaudeville dance kind of rhythm. When the song is sung by a selfassured woman, especially in a vaudeville style, it seemed to fit the changing times. By 1900, women were no longer content with their traditional roles. More and more were entering the workforce, some in professional roles traditionally reserved for men. It was a train that was just now pulling out of the station, starting to gather speed. While Eryk absorbed himself in the music he failed to notice a woman who overheard him and wandered in.

"What's that you're playing?" the woman asked.

"Oh, crap!" Eryk thought. He had better not tell her it was a tune from 1929. If he did, she would think for sure he was nuts.

"Oh, something I just made up."

"Play it again, I like it."

"I'm afraid it's gone from my head already. See if you like this..." Eryk picked a Chopin piece he once had to memorize, the waltz number 11 in G-flat major.

"You play terribly well. Are you Mr. Robert Adams-Buell?"

"No, who is he?"

"The new head of the piano department. He's young but I hear he is very talented and he's establishing a fine reputation for himself.

Do you teach here, or are you a student?" the woman asked.

"Sorry to disappoint you. I'm Ian Larkin, history student and aspiring instructor. I'm here for an interview."

"Let me introduce myself. I'm Ada Saecker, class of 1902."

Eryk suddenly realized who this woman was. Ada Saecker had a distinguished career ahead of her as an opera singer, one of a number of talented singers turned out by Lawrence. Others included Luella Chilson Melius and Emma Patten Hoyt.

"What brings you back to the music department then?"

"I was hoping to find Adams-Buell to see if he would help me rehearse an audition piece before I return to New York on the 22nd. I'm sailing to Europe on the Statendam on the 26th to study in Nuremburg and Berlin. I'm hoping to become an opera singer. I've been studying in Paris the past few years."

"Best of luck then."

"Do you want to play for me?"

"What are you working on?"

"'Mon coeur s'ouvre á ta voix' from 'Sampson et Delila'. Do you think you could play a piano arrangement to accompany me?"

"Let's give it a try."

Her singing was marvelous and professional. She was every bit as talented as Eryk expected her to be.

"Thank you. What position did you apply for?" She asked.

"Instructor in history and English for the spring semester."

"Which one is your specialty?"

"History. That's what my degree is in."

"That's nice. My papa and Uncle Frank are very interested in American and European history. Maybe you can meet them and talk about it when they aren't occupied with their businesses. Why don't you come by tomorrow evening to meet them? My Uncle Herman will be there, too. The address is 659 Lawe Street.

"You can help me practice some more and I can sing for my family. My father is returning today from a meeting of the Wisconsin Funeral Directors Association. He's vice president."

"Then I do hope I won't be meeting him in the prone position."

"That depends on how well you accompany me."

"I will play my best then and look forward to meeting your family."

"Good. I have to skidoo. There's a lot I have to do to get ready for my trip. We'll all be at the 10:30 service at the Methodist Episcopal Church tomorrow morning. If you go you might be able to see us there."

Eryk/Ian checked his watch: 10:05 am. Damn! It stopped. He forgot to wind it again and he couldn't check his phone or his tablet computer, either. Once outside he opened his umbrella and went to find a clock on his way back to the boarding house so he could reset his watch.

Along the way he stopped at Wollman's Bazaar to pick up a book and some magazines to browse. Among the dozens of magazines were "Popular Science" costing fifteen cents, "Life" costing twenty cents, "Ebony" costing a whopping fifty cents, "Collier's" for five cents, "Tip Top Weekly" for youth costing five cents, "Amazing Stories" for twenty cents, "Harpers Weekly, the Journal of Civilization" for ten cents, "Vogue" for ten cents, "The Ladies Home Journal" for ten cents, "The Saturday Evening Post" for five cents, and "Harper's Bazaar".

Books on display included "Hound of the Baskervilles," "The Wonderful Wizard of Oz," "Peter Pan in Kensington Gardens," "Call of the Wild," "The Tale of Peter Rabbit," "Sister Carrie," "The Scarlet Pimpernel," "The Return of Sherlock Holmes," "Where Angels Fear to Tread," "The First Men in the Moon," "Rebecca of Sunnybrook Farm," and a huge selection of dime novels and "women's literature," that is, current, sentimental and historical romantic fiction. Women's books and especially magazines had a marked influence on the attitudes, fashions, morals, attitudes and manners of women of the era.

Back at Mrs. Bowe's, Eryk/Ian settled in for the rest of the day and sat next to the window, reading his bootie from Wollman's.

Saturday's Crescent wasn't out yet. Friday's Crescent reported that the Winnebago Company was opening an office in Appleton with a vacuum for hire. Their machine featured a powerful fifteen horsepower gasoline engine and, for a fee, they would come to anyone's house and use a long hose to vacuum the floors, curtains, and upholstery. There was a complaint that too many intoxicated men were boarding the trolleys, causing a disturbance for the passengers and the conductor. The entertainment column noted that the Harvey Dramatic Company was starting a week of dramatic presentations at the Appleton Theatre on Sunday with "Graustark." Tickets were the usual 15, 25, 35, and 50 cents. An article detailed the plans for the Lusitania which would be departing the next day, meaning today, on its maiden voyage from Liverpool to Sandy Hook, New York City. It was attempting to set a new time record. It was a closely followed story.

After a while, Eryk/Ian took a break, grabbed his umbrella, and slipped over to the Palace Theater at 583 Appleton Street, about a seven-block walk. It featured movies and illustrated songs, charging 5 cents admission with every tenth ticket free. Shows ran every half hour between 2:30 and 4:00 and from 7:30 to 10:00 pm. He wanted to simply throw on some jeans and a sweatshirt, but in these times, people dressed to impress.

* * *

On Sunday, Eryk/Ian toyed with the idea of going to the Methodist Episcopal Church to see the Saecker's, but there were three churches. They probably went to the German church since all three brothers were born in Germany, but he didn't know for sure. Besides, it was another chilly and rainy day with temperatures in the upper sixties, so it could wait for another Sunday.

Instead, it was his turn for a weekly warm bath. Afterwards, rather than risking premature death by straight razor at his own hand, he decided to follow up by finding a barber shop. There were plenty nearby; Eryk/Ian picked Robert Weissgerber on College Avenue. Shaves cost a dime.

After supper he went to his room to again retrieve his umbrella, and prepared to head for Lawe Street. Before he made it to the front door Ada walked in. "My Uncle Frank came to fetch you so you don't have to go out in this bad weather. Honestly, I think he just likes to show off his machine. It's a killer, an '06 Studebaker Tonneau Model F."

"That's kind of him, I'm sure. I can't wait to ride in it."

"Make some appropriate noises. Papa could have sent the hearse," she said as they went to the car.

"If your father did send his hearse, I doubt I'd be in any condition to know about it anyway."

"Have you ridden in an automobile before?"

"Not like your uncle's."

"Uncle Frank, this is Eryk, the young man I told you about. Maybe you can educate him."

"I'm very pleased to meet you Mr. Saecker. Beautiful machine. I've never seen one like it before," a true statement if there was one.

"Danke schön. Please call me Frank. You can't call all of us 'Mr. Saecker' ya know. Some people in this town complain about the automobiles and say they're a danger to the horses and pedestrians. They complain about the traffic jams, ya know? We have some speeders who race down the street at ten miles an hour, but we're dealing with 'em. I'll tell you what the real problem is, though: it's bicycles. They mow down the pedestrians on the sidewalks. I'm sure y'u've seen it. Accidents almost every day."

"I have seen a few close calls." It seemed that quite a few residents of Appleton spoke at least a little German. Eryk/Ian wasn't one of them.

"Uncle Herman is a Fire and Police Commissioner. He's deciding what should be done," Ada interjected.

"Have ya met anyone else since ya got here?" Uncle Frank asked.

"I ran into Edna Ferber and Byron Beveridge at the Crescent office."

"Ya', the lunachick. Byron's a regular guy and mixes pretty well, but Ferber resents us, nicht wahr? Ya notice she wears simple clothes and she's suspicious of any'n who dress real fancy and has lots o' money."

"I see. She didn't seem too fond of me, either. Asked a lot of questions."

"Probably her reporter habit. Always looking for a story," Ada said.

"Here we are. Please come in and make y'urself at home," Frank said. "I understand the two of ya will be entertaining us t'night."

"Your niece certainly will and I'll try my best."

Ada introduced Ian to her father, who preferred to be called William, and to her Uncle Hermann. The three surviving Saecker brothers were partners and prominent businessmen in Appleton.

"Let me show ya ar house," William Saecker offered. It was a finely furnished house indeed, with all the latest conveniences. In the early 1900s possessions implied status and the Saeckers had plenty of both.

Of course, the house had indoor plumbing and electric service. Appleton was a progressive city. It had the world's first central hydroelectric generating plant in 1882, the first successful electric street car in 1886, the first telephone system in Wisconsin in 1877, and the first home ever with electric lighting west of Mississippi in 1882.

The Saecker house had electric lights as well as fans to keep it cool in the summer.

"We have an electric sewing machine, ar own telephone, a stereoscope, a phonograph and a collection o' disks o' course, but we have an electric iron and an electric toaster. I'm lookin' into the purchase of an electric washing machine. New electrical appliances are being invented all da time. T'ere are commercial air conditioning and dishwashing machines t'ese days, but nothing we can get for ar home yet."

"May I ask how your businesses are doing?" Eryk/Ian inquired.

"Booming. I have forty employees in the machine shop now and we're expandin' the furniture business, too. The undertakin' business takes care of itself, 'specially since the population is growin'.

"Wit' the interurban and shorts people can come ta us from all over. We can get materials from farther away now, too, and we ship all over the country. In fact, with trains, steamers, and ferries the people here travel anywhere in the country and abroad now. Airships and airplanes will be addin' to that."

"T'is is the best time to be an American. It's the greatest country the world has ever seen. People have been callin' it 'The American Century' for more than ten years now and properly so. Anybody who's willin' ta work hard can make a success of it these days," Hermann added.

Their optimism was contagious. Eryk could easily exchange some of his modern conveniences and instant communications for the relaxing simplicity, opportunity, and less frantic pace of life. The biggest drawbacks in his mind were the lack of antibiotics and unsophisticated medical knowledge of the time.

"Papa is leading the effort to modernize the library and improve education here in the city, He's president of the Outagamie County Board of Libraries and they've established scholarship funds at Lawrence," Ada said proudly.

"Do you care for some desert?" William asked. "We have strudel wit' tea or beer if y'u'd rather."

"Thank you. That sounds good. I'll have some tea."

"Will ya be here for the World Pure Food Exposition in Chicago between November sixteenth and twenty-third?" Frank asked.

"If Lawrence offers me a position."

"People want to eat healthy these days so it's a good thing."

"Time for me to entertain you," Ada interrupted. "Ian, do you think you can read a piano score of 'O zittre nicht, mein lieber Sohn' from Mozart's 'Die Zauberflöte' and then we can do the Saint Saens? Naturally I need a German audition piece since I'm going there".

"Piece of cake. I'd like to warm up first with a little piece I'm dedicating to Uncle Frank." He then proceeded to play "In my Merry Oldsmobile" because he didn't know the music to "In my Merry Studebaker." Ada and Uncle Frank joined in as soon as they recognized the tune.

After that, he accompanied Ada singing her two arias.

Strangely enough, Ada received a standing ovation from her father and uncles for her efforts.

"It's time for me to be leaving," Eryk/Ian said. "Thanks for the hospitality."

"We were happy to have ya visit us. Y'u'll have to stop by sometime when it's not raining to see the garden in back."

"I will be pleased to drive ya back to y'ur boardin' house," Frank offered. "No point catchin' a cold in this rain."

"Thank you so much. Will you drop me off at the Union News Depot on College Avenue? I want to pick up copies of the Evening Crescent and the Daily Post."

"Certainly, I can stop along the way," Frank replied.

Both newspapers had ads for The Fox River Valley (Appleton) Fair to start on Monday which was registration day. Tuesday would be farmer's day, Wednesday was Appleton day, and Thursday was Children's Day. The State Fair in Milwaukee was also that week from the ninth through the thirteenth.

Eryk noticed that most of the ads carried a business address but only some included a phone number. There were ads for train fares in the Post nearly every day. Round trip fares between Chicago and New York or Boston on the New York Central were six dollars. One-way fares to California, Utah, or Colorado on the Chicago, Milwaukee, and St. Paul Railroad were seven dollars. One-way fares to San Francisco, Los Angeles, Oregon, or Washington on the Chicago and Northwestern were also seven dollars.

* * *

Byron Beveridge already knew from talking to Larkin that he arrived around midday on Wednesday and was staying at Mrs. Bowe's boarding house. Figuring Larkin would have traveled north from Chicago on the Chicago and Northwestern, he found out from the railway that the conductor from the Wednesday mid-morning arriving train would be at the Appleton again that Monday morning. He hopped on the train and found the conductor as soon as it pulled into the station, since one of the perks of his press pass allowed him to ride for free.

"Sir, I'm Byron Beveridge, a reporter for the Crescent, and I'm lookin' for a man named Ian Larkin who disembarked here last Wednesday morning. He was from Kentucky lookin' for an instructor position at Lawrence College and would be stayin' at a boarding house on Lawrence Street. Did ya by any chance happen to talk to such a man or overhear him?"

"Ah do seem to recall a feller askin' if ah knew the way tah Lawrence and Morrison Streets."

"What else did he say? Do ya recall what he looked like?"

"Didn't say nothin' much else as ah recall. Seems tah me he needed a shave, coupla days' growth. Brown suit, brown hair, black tie maybe, ah'm not sure. Maybe mid-twenties. Big beat up ol' suitcase."

"Anything else ya noticed then?"

"Nah, that's about it."

"What'd ya tell 'im then?"

"Didn't know how fer he had tah go an' to take a horse-cab tah be sure."

"Thanks." Beveridge had to hurry and hop back off the train. Now he could ask the horse-cab drivers that were there that morning if they were also there Wednesday and saw anyone matching that description. None had.

Was this Ian Larkin? It had to be. How many could have disembarked Wednesday to go to Lawrence and Morrison? There could only be one except by an extraordinary coincidence.

He inquired at the ticket office, the telegraph office, and the station manager's office if they had seen Larkin but none had. Then he asked at the newsstand. "Carl, I'm lookin' for a man that was here last Wednesday mornin' from the sout'. He's lookin for a job at Lawrence University and was headin' for a boarding house on Lawrence Street. Did ya see him?"

"Ya sure did. I remember 'cause he had a funny accent. Didn't know what tah make of it. He was lookin' for newspapers an' we talked some baseball."

"That's him. What did he look like then?"

"Dark blue t'ree piece suit, blue tie, walkin' stick, couple o' old suitcases, mid or late twenties, dark hair, square jaw."

"Thanks, that's what I needed."

Were there somehow two different Ian Larkins? Of course, there couldn't be. Something happened at the train station that morning. Beveridge went to talk to the station manager.

"Zach, looks to me like there was some incident here last Wednesday morning. What do ya know?"

"Nothin' I can recall."

"Any arguments, fights, accidents, anything then?"

"Nothin' out of the ordinary."

"Did ya find anything outa place, blood somewhere, old clothes layin' about, suitcases not belongin' ta anyone?"

"Not a thing."

"So strange."

One Ian Larkin got off the train, a different Ian Larkin went to the boarding house. Maybe it was simple, the conductor got it wrong or the brown suit was someone else who just happened to be going the same way as Larkin. Or, maybe something untoward happened, something newsworthy, but what? Was there a plan, the two of them agreed to change places? Did the blue suit lure the brown suit somewhere and do him in? Were they making an alibi for each other while they carried out a swindle or a crime?

Beveridge wanted to find the brown suit man. That was the key to this mystery. His next step was to ask Mrs. Bowe if someone in a brown suit also registered Wednesday or if anyone saw a man in the neighborhood wearing a brown suit.

Chapter Seven
New Pleasures

Monday dawned a fine day, around seventy degrees and sunny and Eryk/Ian didn't intend to waste it.

In the news, the Grocer's annual convention was commencing in the morning with the usual round of speeches, including one by the Appleton mayor, and reports from various officers and committees. It would be followed in the evening by a ball at Harmonie Hall at 672 Morrison on the corner at Fisk Street. Eryk/Ian decided not to crash it.

Today was Eryk/Ian's next-to-last chance to try out one of the grand pianos at Lawrence before the semester commenced and they were no longer available to him. Classical standards would be best to play on such fine instruments. Rags, waltzes, polkas, and other popular fare would be better on the old beat up upright at the boarding house. He had sheet music for Beethoven's "Moonlight Sonata" and the Chopin Nocturne in E-flat major, and those would do for a start.

The next thing Eryk/Ian knew, he had an audience.

"Ya play very well. Are ya on the faculty?" a woman asked in a bright, cheerful, interested voice. She was ordinary in appearance, with brown hair in the Edwardian hairstyle that was fashionable at the time, brown eyes, and maybe early to mid-twenties Eryk thought.

"No, I'm scheduled for an interview in a few weeks for an instructor position."

"Y'u're awfully early ya know. Do ya intend to keep playing the piano until they call ya?"

"Can't. My fingers are wearing down too fast. I came early so I could prepare. I wanted to learn as much as I could about the school and the town." Eryk was obsessively thorough. It was one of the reasons Trice hired him, but what about Ian? After all, he failed the interview. Should Eryk intentionally blow it, as much as that would go against his nature?

"That's very commendable of ya. Don't worry you'll love it here and I know you'll do well at y'ur interview. I can see you are smart and determined. What do I call ya?"

"I'm Ian Larkin from Kentucky."

"And I'm Vera Bleecker from Wisconsin. Pleased to meet ya."

It seemed to Eryk the upper Midwest accent was noticeably more pronounced now than in his time. When Vera spoke it, it was irresistible.

"Are you a student?"

"I am and so is my brother Lyell. I'm waitin' for him to meet me here."

"What's your major? Are you a music student?"

"I'm majoring in geography but I'm here to make sure I'm on the list for the Aeolis Ladies Chorus again this year. What about you? Do ya sing as well as play'?"

"Yes, and at the same time, but somehow they usually come out in different keys. What part do you sing?"

"First alto. How about you?"

"Depends on what I had for breakfast. I can sing first alto if the fruit was sour enough. Is your brother older or younger?"

"Younger. He's a freshman here. I'm takin' him under my wing 'till he's comfortable with the place. He's only eighteen."

"What year are you?"

"I'm a sophomore."

"You're only a year older then."

"I'll be twenty-three next month. I got a late start. My mother moved here last year so Lyell and I could go ta Lawrence."

"What about your father?" Eryk could see how sad she suddenly looked. "I'm sorry, I shouldn't have asked about him."

"That's alright. He died in '89 when I was only four. Harrie, I mean Lyell, that's what he wants to be called now, was only eight months old and my other brother Leslie was barely three. Lyell was named after him. My father's name was Harry. Ya know, I'm the only one who remembers my father. My brothers were too young."

"I can tell you miss him a lot. I'm sorry your father couldn't be there for you. I lost my mother when I was young, too, but my father always took good care of me."

Eryk was strongly drawn to this woman. Now he felt awful, like a con man and a fake and in fact, that is exactly what he was. A sociopath or con artist would think nothing of presenting a false persona for the purposes of manipulating the unsuspecting, in fact, that is their modus operandi. Healthier individuals want to be known and appreciated for who they actually are, or more accurately, for who they perceive themselves to be.

Vera was outgoing and engaging. Eryk desperately wanted to be authentic. Well, suppose he did tell her his real story, that he was a time traveler from the future? She would run away screaming "Lunatic!" at the top of her lungs.

What if he proved to her who he really was? That would change history, of course. Everyone and anyone would be after him, begging, coercing, flattering, manipulating, befriending him and wanting to know the future so they could take advantage of it.

Either he was a con man or a mass murderer of the future unborn; being honest and genuine was not an option. Eryk had no choice but to destroy his own soul through some form of dishonesty. That would be his situation for the entire duration of his stay. He could walk away from this particular encounter, but that was turning out to be so very difficult to do.

"Is y'ur family from the sout' then?"

"No, my parents came over from Wales."

"Ya mean you're Welch? That makes us neighbors. My mother's parents were both Scottish."

"What about your father's side?"

"Dutch. The Bleeckers settled in Canada but my grandfather moved to the U.S. when he was young."

"What do you think about going to college with your brother?"

"We're both lookin' forward to it. I have a close-knit family but Lyell and I are especially so. What about you? Any family nearby?"

"No, none. What else do you do at Lawrence besides sing?"

"Whatever I want. There are plenty of choices. They want ya to participate in physical culture, but that's more for my brothers. They're both nuts about football. Lyell plans to try out for the team."

"Is he any good?"

"Of course, smarty."

"Do you follow the sports here?"

"I have to. My brother will see to it. Besides, I'm in one of the literary societies that publishes the Lawrentian, the weekly campus paper. It's topical."

"So, you know all the latest gossip around here?"

"I have the word on absolutely everybody. If ya get a job here I'll know every scrap of gossip about *you*, too. Don't expect for a minute ya can hide y'ur secrets from me."

"I'm impressed. Do I confess right here and now or will you give me time to reconsider my many dark secrets first?"

"Ya'd better write them down for me. Otherwise, I'm afraid y'u'll forget some of 'em, the juiciest ones."

"I'd like to see your brother play football sometime."

In fact, Eryk did want to see a football game, college, high school, amateur, professional, any kind. If Lawrence played a game before he had to go back to his own time, he would watch it. It would be interesting because the game was different in 1907. The field was 110 yards long. Teams had only three downs to make ten yards. Field goals were four points and touchdowns were five. The forward pass had been allowed starting the prior year, but there was a fifteen-yard penalty for incompletions and no passing was allowed inside an opponent's twenty-yard line. Kickoffs were from midfield. One other thing: football was dangerous. The previous year nine high school and two college players were killed while ninety-eight others were seriously injured.

"I'll let ya know when he's playing," Vera replied.

"I'm going to the fair tomorrow," Eryk/Ian blurted out. "Do you and your brother want to come?"

"Sorry, Lyell will still be registering and I'll help him. There's a dance at Koehn's Hall tomorrow night. It's on Richmond Street at eight o'clock. Do ya wanna ask me to go?"

"Will you go to the dance at with me tomorrow evening at Koehn's Hall?"

"I'd be delighted to if my mother will allow me. Ya do dance don't ya?"

"I can fake it but I don't know any of your northern dances. Will you show me the steps tomorrow?" Well, Eryk did know how to dance but he certainly didn't know the two-step, the cakewalk, the new waltz, the polka, the castle step, or the other dances that were popular then.

"I'm pleased to show ya. We have a phone. I'll write down my phone number for ya. Where ya stayin'?"

"The Bowe House on Lawrence."

"We're in a different direction from the school on Meade Street, four blocks from the park."

This was getting dangerous. Eryk knew better than to get involved. He was supposed to be strictly an observer. He knew he had to minimize contact with people of this era but he couldn't help himself. Maybe it was pre-destined. Wasn't this the woman who found Ian's journal?

Lyell asked Vera on their way out, "Who is that fellow?"

"He hopes to be an instructor here next semester. Sign up for his class if he makes it and I'll convince him to give ya an 'A'."

"Do you like him?"

"Maybe he could be a friend of ours. His eyes remind me of father and he has the same sense of purpose. I like having a friend who's a few years older."

"Your new boyfriend then."

"Never. Don't say that. I don't want a boyfriend right now." After supper Eryk tried to clear his mind with that day's Crescent and Post. The Crescent published the music for "Molly in the Ballet" so he gave it a half-hearted rendition in the parlor.

The papers reported on the fair and on the progress of the Lusitania. The Crescent reported on a reduction in transatlantic fares. Eastbound rates were cut to between $22.50 and $77.50 depending on the steamship and the class of service. Eryk thought about Vera and put away the papers. He wasn't terribly interested in the news that evening.

* * *

Tuesday dawned with a light rain with temperatures headed for the upper sixties, nothing that would stop Eryk/Ian. After breakfast he grabbed his umbrella and headed for the trolley. The fairgrounds were at the west end of College Avenue, only a short walk from one of the stops. It would be a very busy day. He decided to wait to call Vera until he returned. Maybe she would call off the dance first so he wouldn't have to.

Farmer's day at the Fox River Valley Fair saw meager crowds. A major attraction was the three horse races each day commencing at 2:00. Sixty horses were entered for the week. There were nearly continuous vaudeville shows, moving pictures, bands and music all day, a burlesque show, a Japanese bowling alley, a merry-go-round, a curio shop, a photo button gallery, a ring toss, a wheel-of-fortune, a jewelry spindle, and doll racks. Prizes were being given for poultry, cows, bulls, hogs, dairy products, and baked goods. Tuesday would also feature the judging of cattle, horses, hogs, and sheep. More than a hundred sales booths along "The Pike" peddled hats, butter and cheese, meat, vegetables, and furniture among other things. Eryk/Ian expected to see a booth for the Saecker Brothers South Kaukauna or the Saecker and Rogers College Avenue Furniture and Undertaking Company.

When Eryk/Ian returned to the boarding house he found a message to call Vera under his door. He went to the Wisconsin Telephone Company on College Avenue to make the call.

"My mother wants to meet ya and see if she approves of ya before ya take me to the dance tonight," she told him. "I'll convince her she approves, so ya better dress up and don't make me look like a simp. Lyell will be going with us. Looks like ya need a chaperone. I better watch out for you ain'a?"

"Yes, you had. As a matter of fact, I ran out of paper listing all my terrible dark secrets for your gossip file. I'm looking forward to getting to know both of you better, but don't you think it will be awkward, the three of us dancing together at the same time?"

"Not at all. That's the three-step. It's the new dance craze."

"Then you'd better allow me an extra half hour to learn that one."

"Y'u'll catch on. I have a ten o'clock curfew. Is that alright with you?"

"I wouldn't have it any other way."

"Pick me up at seven thirty and make your best impression."

"Don't worry."

Eryk/Ian wore his best suit and vest with a plain blue tie and slicked his hair back imitating the popular style. Vera looked pretty in a frilly white shirtwaist with a high neck, leather boots with buttons, a blue bell-shaped skirt, a wide brimmed hat with ribbons and bows, and her same Edwardian hairstyle newly individualized with ringlets around her ears. Lyell wore a dark grey suit and vest. This was a time when people's status was judged by the way they dressed and the manner in which they spoke, and the Bleeckers were leaving nothing to chance.

From the house on Meade Street, it was a nine-block walk to the dance. That left them only a little over an hour, but that was fine with Eryk/Ian. She would be busy with the start of classes and school activities the next month or two and it wouldn't be wise to interfere with that. He was content to spend an hour or so with her and to meet her family. He knew he was going too far and he should stop this budding relationship immediately, but he couldn't help himself.

"Have you thought about what you want to do after you graduate?" he asked her.

"Travel. I want to see the world, don't you? Not just this country. I want to visit my mother's side of the family in Scotland. Then I want to see all of Great Britain. And France. I want to see Europe."

"Would you ever want to want to live in Europe, too?"

"Oh, no. I expect I'll teach somewhere not too far from here. Teaching is one of the few professions open to women, ya know. I can travel on school breaks. Lyell wants to teach too, like his older sister."
"You don't have to teach unless it's what you really want. More and more women are entering other professions these days. You can teach at the college level, or be a reporter or some other professional."

"I'll decide that. I don't want to waste my energy fighting for pay and promotions when there's a clear path somewhere, 'n so?"

"Well then, it sounds like you know what you want."

"That's right. Ya wanna teach yourself or else why are ya here?"

"I want to teach subjects that interest me but I especially want the chance to do research."

"You should go to the Lawrence library tomorrow if y'u're serious. Read the Ariel yearbooks, find out who the teachers and the bigshots are around there. Get the back copies of the Lawrentian, find out what the students like and see what they think."

"I'll look for your gossip columns."

"What a wisenheimer. Ya could irritate me if I let ya."

"Sorry, you're much too sweet for that."

"So true. Do ya know the two-step? I'll show ya." Before they knew it, it was 9:30.

"Thank you for teaching me the dance steps," Eryk said. "We'd better get going. I don't want to break your curfew and have your mother lock me out." All during the past hour whenever Eryk/Ian held Vera's hand it was warm to the touch.

"There's a bright comet in the sky Thursday. Maybe we can see it together if the sky is clear," she said.

"Around nine o'clock?"

"If it's visible then. Meet me at the observatory. I'm sure some other students and professors will be there, too."

"I'll look for you then. I can't wait. It will be fun."

"I'm goin' ta find Lyell so we can skidoo. Thank ya so much for the dance. I had a wonderful time."

"I enjoyed every minute with you. Can't wait until Thursday."

Comets have been seen as an omen, often a bad one, throughout the centuries. He hoped it wasn't a bad omen for Eryk or Ian.

* * *

Wednesday morning brought still another rainy day, in fact, it was a soaking rain accompanied by temperatures of around seventy. It was the first day of classes at Lawrence. Eryk/Ian decided it was time to give his umbrella a break and just stay put. He would spend most of the day indoors reading his books and magazines.

At around six o'clock Eryk/Ian headed for Griffin's Restaurant to eat and stretch his legs. The corner table he preferred was free, so he went over and sat down. Before long Karen brought him coffee. "How's my best customer today?"

"In great need of swimming lessons. How about you?"

"Hangin'. I have a life jacket. Here is our menu f'r today."

"What's the daily special?"

"Spaghetti with a roll and butter f'r ten cents but I recommend the veal cutlet with mushroom sauce, bread and butter f'r twenty cents or our poached eggs with rice and curry sauce and bread and butter f'r two bits."

"Thanks, I'll go with the cutlet special."

"Comin' right up."

"Tell me Karen, are the women in this town always so friendly and welcoming, or is it my accent they like?"

"Don't ya know? Y'u're the Gibson man. They all want to take care of ya."

"What do you mean?"

"Everybody loves the Gibson girl, especially the man in the drawings, but he can't have her. He always falls short. That's why he looks so sad and wistful. He's always in mournin' over the girl he can never have. You look like the man in the drawings. Both of you are dark-haired, square-jawed, neat, clean-shaven, and misty-eyed."

"I see. I'd better work on changing my countenance."

"Don't worry. I'll always talk to ya no matter who y'u're like."

Eryk/Ian was greeted by Mrs. Bowe when he returned to his room after dinner.

"A Mr. Beveridge was just here from the Crescent lookin' for ya. He said the two of ya had supper plans. He wanted to know if ya ever had any visitors or phone calls and who ya made friends with here. I told him ya just keep to y'urself."

"Thank you for that. What's always on my mind is the fine fare you'll be serving for breakfast and dinner tomorrow. It's something I've learned to look forward to." It looked like the cat and mouse game was underway with Beveridge and Eryk/Ian wanted it to stop.

"Oh, ya flatter me too much," the landlady responded.

The papers that day recorded that Lusitania was steaming at 23.5 knots and could break the record time for the Liverpool to New York Atlantic crossing, "A Soldier of the Empire" was being presented at the Appleton Theatre, there was a Butchers Dance at Harmonie Hall, and a boxing and wrestling program opened at 8:00 that evening featuring Illinois welterweight champion Ted Tonneman. Tuesday's Crescent had an article that began "The automobile is the new means of escape for burglars." The Post reported that a committee was trying to organize a Valley League of baseball teams from the nearby communities. Both papers reported that because of the rain, the Fox River Valley Fair was extended by another day so all of the horse races and events could be held.

When Eryk/Ian went downstairs later, his selection for the evening was Debussy's Arabesque number 1. Fortunately, Beveridge hadn't returned.

* * *

Eryk/Ian doubted the comet would be visible on Thursday but the weather was spectacular, clear and eighty degrees. The comet would in fact be clearly visible that night at a predicted brightness of magnitude two.

Around five thirty he headed to Griffin's for supper. Karen greeted him. "How's my favorite customer?"

"How's my favorite waitress? But I know everyone calls you that."

"Did ya know a reporter from the Crescent was asking about ya this afternoon? He said somethin' about an ax murderer."

"Is that a gag?"

"I thought so, but is there somethin' ya wanna confess?"

"No, nothing exciting going on. What did he say?"

"He said if ya get a job at Lawrence he wants tah do an article about the new teacher in town and what ya think about Appleton."

"Seems like that's the big question on everybody's mind. That was Byron Beveridge?"

"The very same."

"He's been trying to have supper with me for a while now. I told him I wouldn't be a fit subject for public consumption and he should drop the whole idea of writing an article."

"I don't think he will. He likes to ask a lot o' questions."

"Speaking of public consumption, what do you recommend tonight?"

"We have sliced chicken with spinach an' toast f'r two bits."

"That sounds fine."

Eryk/Ian's musical selection for the night was Debussy's version of "Clair de Lune."

It didn't calm he nerves. He remained worried, what if Beveridge or Ferber found Ian's aunt in New York City? They might find out things about Ian that Eryk didn't know and the jig would be up. But how will they find her? There was no forebears.com in 1907. The Crescent wasn't about to send a key reporter to Kentucky or New York on a hunch. No relatives were mentioned in Ian's father's obituary, although Ian must have known his aunt's name.

Eryk knew the reporters sensed a story. They couldn't possibly know it was one of the biggest stories of the decade. As long as Eryk/Ian kept his mouth shut, how could they ever guess the truth without everyone calling them crazy? But how could he be sure he wouldn't accidently say or do something to spill the beans? There is too much buried in the human psyche, too much that is unconscious, too much shadow that is ready to project itself somewhere without conscious awareness. Eryk was more and more worried.

Chapter Eight
The Omen

Thursday evening remained clear. Eryk went to the observatory early and walked around the campus for a while partly to get some exercise, but mostly to avoid Beveridge. Didn't he have plenty of other stories to report on?

Sunset was around six o'clock (there was no daylight savings time in 1907) and twilight ended around 7:00. Eryk arrived at the observatory at 6:30, keeping one eye on the sky and the other scanning for Vera and Lyell. There were maybe a dozen students and faculty milling about. Finally, he spotted Vera shortly before seven. There was no sign of Lyell.

"I'm so pleased you could make it," Eryk/Ian said. "The paper says the comet will be visible in the west. It will set soon after the sun." During the previous two months or so, Daniel's comet had been visible right before sunrise or else it was hidden behind the sun. "Where's Lyell?"

"Busy. He'll come later if he can."

So, they sat there together as the sun and crescent moon sank beyond view, with the stars and prophetic comet gradually materializing. It seemed for a minute like it was only the two of them quietly suspended beneath the Milky Way.

"Can you wish upon a comet?" Vera asked. "Is it bright enough for that? My wish is that you get a teaching position here."

"Vera, if I don't get a position I'll have to leave. We shouldn't be getting involved until I know for sure. I think I made a mistake asking you out."

"Don't worry about it, silly. Besides, I asked *you* to meet me here. I just want to spread my wings and have fun while I'm at Lawrence. I won't take this seriously if you don't. Are ya planin' to show me a good time, no strings attached?"

"Whenever you like."

"Why don't ya help Lyell and me with our homework on Saturday real quick? We can meet in City Park if it's nice."

"That's your idea of a good time?"

"You betcha. Isn't studying history always loads of fun?"

With that, she kissed him lightly on his cheek. Worse yet, he returned the kiss.

"Don't worry," she said. "And besides, y'u'll get the job. Lawrence is crazy if they don't gobble ya up."

Of course, Eryk knew he would be leaving and it wasn't fair to Vera. He hated having to stick to his story. He wanted to stop pretending and be Eryk, and have a genuine relationship.

They watched until the comet dimmed in the thick low sky. It soon disappeared behind some buildings. Nearby, a professor was explaining what comets were and why they grew tails to three students.

"Quite a sight," Eryk/Ian said. "Bright comets don't come around that often. I think the next one will be Halley in 1910."

"Then I'll meet ya here again in '10. I have to leave now. There are vampires about and I don't want my mother to think y'u're one of them."

"You're safe 'till next time. I had my fill of blood before you got here. It was a lot more crowded than this when I arrived but I took care of it."

"Very funny. Vampires are only dangerous when there's a full moon or a comet."

"Well, the moon is waxing now, you know, so you have to be very careful. What a nice smile you have. You must be looking forward to becoming an immortal vampire yourself."

"Ya, maybe I'm one already. You make me feel special, like y'u've already bitten me."

"Please don't tell your mother that. Vera, I wanted to ask you, I'm going to see "The District Leader" on Sunday. It would be great if you wanted to accompany me. The moon won't be full yet."

"I'll see what my mother has to say. Sundays are family days, but I'm inclined to go anyway."

"I hope you can. I'll have something to look forward to."

Eryk/Ian was thankful Vera was busy with school and extracurricular activities and he wouldn't be seeing her for the next several days. He just couldn't summon up the moral strength to stop.

That evening the Post reported that outdoor sleeping was the latest health fad in Appleton, while the Crescent stated that the night watchman at a brewery saw a ghost. Why was it the night watchman at the Temperance Society never saw one? A freight train engineer on the Rock Island Railroad went berserk and opened the throttle of his heavy train all the way. The train tore down the track at a frightening speed, in danger of derailment, reaching more than six miles an hour before the fireman and head brakeman could subdue the engineer and slow it down. On the most widely followed story, the Lusitania was on a pace to break the transatlantic crossing record of just under five days.

Vera was still on Eryk/Ian's mind. After glancing at the paper in his room he went downstairs. The other boarders had the pleasure of hearing him play Satie's "Je te Veux."

* * *

Friday the thirteenth was another fine day, clear and in the upper seventies. Vera was busy at school and Eryk/Ian had to plan his day.

There was no television, no internet, no mobile phones, and no commercial radio broadcasts, although the first transatlantic radio transmission had been in 1901. Only a few people saw radio's potential, some of them newspaper publishers alarmed at the possible competition for paying advertisements.

Both local and out-of-town newspapers were easy to find, and new additions of news magazines came out weekly or monthly. There was no breaking news, just extra editions of the newspapers. Compared to instant internet news and events, it felt like there was a paucity of information. Eryk was used to dialing up anyone, anytime, so life in 1907 was a Darwinian experience. At least the slower pace of life was very refreshing.

There was plenty of entertainment, though, and it was all live. You just weren't going to see it sitting on a couch, and much of it was participatory: socials, dances, sports, amusement and trolley parks, dinners, auctions, community events, choirs and soloists, musical performances, and the like. The most popular form of entertainment was vaudeville, though movies would soon overtake it. Reading was popular as were dramatic readings. Almost every house had a piano and a stereoscope, and many owned a phonograph, which cost anywhere from $7.50 for an Edison "Gem" to $125 or more for an ornate Victrola floor model. Telephones were becoming more and more common, elevating the sport of gossip; an estimated 13 to 25% of households had a phone, roughly half of which were party lines.

Trains, trolleys and inter-urbans were frequent and cheap. Appleton town folk regularly travelled to Chicago, Milwaukee, Oshkosh, Green Bay, St. Paul, and other cities for shopping, Grand Opera, orchestra concerts, plays, and special events such as a circus, a ballgame, or maybe a Wild West show. Round trip fare to Oshkosh, for example, a favorite shopping destination, was twenty cents.

There were also more than thirty organizations or individual chapters for men and women. Men could join the Foresters, Knights of Columbus, Knights of Pythias, Masons, Odd Fellows, Woodmen, and numerous others. There were nine women's clubs in Appleton, including auxiliaries of some of the men's clubs and others such as the

Eastern Star. These organizations regularly sponsored charitable activities, dances, dinners, educational functions, parades, and picnics.

The primary social havens for men were the saloon and the barber shop.

Entertainers toured the country in the form of vaudeville, medicine shows, dramatic and operatic companies, circuses, shows, and individual acts. Any town of any size had at least one opera house, and most had an auditorium or playhouse.

So it was that in the afternoon, Eryk/Ian decided to take a trolley to the Bijou Theater at 625 Oneida Street to take in a vaudeville show. The day's acts were typical: Espe, Dutton, and Espe with juggling and comedy on their unicycles; Jack Younger, the specimen of physical development; Miss Kirkley, soprano; and sketch plays and comedy acts. The theater featured "continuous vaudeville afternoon and evening."

Upon his return, Eryk/Ian's piano piece for the evening was "Give My Regards to Broadway" by George M. Cohan. In those days, with no radio or television and no high-fidelity recordings, it wasn't the singers but rather the song writers who were the rock stars. That included Cohan, one of the first and most prolific of them all, Stephen Foster, and numerous others.

In Friday's news, six thousand attended Children's Day at the fair, including twenty-five hundred paid (since children were admitted free). A hundred and eighty-three freshmen enrolled at Lawrence College, the most ever. The school decided to expand its football team to at least thirty players. In other news the Fair lost $800 for the week, which was blamed on the rain Tuesday and Wednesday. The Lusitania arrived at Sandy Hook after an Atlantic crossing lasting five days fifty-four minutes at an average speed of twenty-eight miles an hour. Men were leaving to take advantage of high construction wages in the

Panama Canal Zone despite the prevalence of malaria and other tropical diseases. An Albany youth planned to go over Niagara Falls in a barrel.

Eryk/Ian decided to walk the mile and a half east to the village of Little Chute, in the direction of Kaukauna, and wander around to see what was there. The locks and dams that attempted to tame the river and make it navigable were of special interest. On his return, he took the interurban back to Appleton and then boarded the trolley along College Avenue. When he got to Appleton Street, he walked the rest of the way to the Appleton Theatre box office. Tickets started at 25 cents, but he went all out and bought two box seat tickets in anticipation of Sunday, for $1.50 each.

* * *

Sunday finally came, a clear and pleasant if rather warm day in the mid-eighties. Eryk/Ian had been impatiently looking forward to seeing Vera again for the past three days. She asked him to wait for her at the theater that evening. It was ten blocks away for her, a bit closer for Eryk/Ian. The show was a musical revue boasting fifty performers and twelve hit songs.

"This is a treat for me. I'm happy we can be together tonight," he told her. "I bought box seats just for this occasion."

"Box seats? I'm sorry, that's much too extravagant," she said. Ordinary people had budgets and were careful with their spending. "I never had box seats ta anything. That's a lot o' scratch."

"Anything for you. I enjoy your company so much I wanted to make the most out of our evening together." Now Eryk/Ian was embarrassed but what could he do?

"That's nice of ya. I don't wanna hurt your feelin's but it's awfully expensive. My family is very thrifty, ya know. They'd never spend so much on entertainment. Please don't say anything ta Lyell or my mother."

"Don't worry, just enjoy it. Your family has done very well for itself."

They went inside to claim their seats. She leaned over and rested her head on his shoulder while they waited for the entertainment to commence.

"What do you think of your classes and your teachers this year?"

"I'm in Miss Lillian Lowell's Expression class. That's a course I really wanted. I like my English and geography classes, too. Voice lessons are fun but it's hard. There are some good singers around here."

"I wish we could sit like this all night."

"If we did, I'd have to write about it. Next semester when ya get the job I plan to write all about the new history and English instructor. Give me a good juicy story or I'll make one up."

"I'll give you a tale nobody will believe."

"When I'm through with my article everybody will want either y'ur head or y'ur autograph."

"Which one will it be then?"

"Depends on how ya treat me."

"Isn't it a lot of work putting out a newspaper on a regular schedule?"

"Not really. There's almost sixty of us working on the Lawrentian, from four clubs. I'm specializin' in the sophomore class. Lyell doesn't know it yet, but he's going to be my freshman class spy. Freshmen *have* to obey the sophomores ya know. It's a rule."

"I didn't know Lawrence offered a major in espionage."

"You betcha and I'm the department chair."

"I see. My lips are now sealed for the rest of the evening."

"It feels good ta be together."

"And you brighten up my day. Everyone's day. I'm so happy your mother approved that you came."

That night Eryk/Ian's musical selection was "To a Wild Rose" by MacDowell.

* * *

In the news there was still another auto accident caused by a partially buried lead pipe some farmers placed across a road. They were fed up with automobiles scaring their animals.

It rained all the next week Monday through Friday, drizzle on Monday but heavy rain on Tuesday, limiting what Eryk/Ian could do. Temperatures were in the seventies and eighties. Vera was busy at school, although the three of them did arrange to meet for homework for an hour on Wednesday at 4:00, after Dr. Plantz's 3:00 pm prayer session.

On Tuesday the heavily advertised "The Flaming Arrow" was at the Appleton Theatre, but Eryk decided not to go. Instead, he went people-watching at Pettibone-Peabody and some of the other department stores. He also picked up another slew of magazines to look through the rest of the week, part of his quest to get the feel of life in the early nineteen hundreds.

After his all too brief time with Vera and Harry on Wednesday, Eryk/Ian decided to treat himself to "The Irish Pawnbrokers" with Murphy, Murphy, and Murphy, and a cast of twenty performers at the Appleton Theatre. This time, he went for a thirty-five-cent seat.

On Thursday and Friday, the twenty-first Wisconsin Infantry held its twenty-second annual reunion in Appleton. A hundred and six of two hundred fifty survivors attended. Thursday's program included speeches, eulogies, and ceremonies. A memorial service was held at the Appleton Theatre in the afternoon. Beveridge was likely to cover the event and leave Ian alone.

In other news, the papers reported that Ryan High School's enrollment was down to 58 seniors, 62 juniors, 93 sophomores and 107 freshmen because more students were enrolling in parochial schools. Men's fashions were looser fitting this year, so older tight clothes were out. In baseball news, on Friday Pittsburgh's Nick Maddox no-hit the Brooklyn Dodgers 2-1.

Finally in the news, Professor Pickering announced that something definitely lives and grows on the moon, though he could not yet say what it was.

Beveridge stopped by the boarding house Friday afternoon. It wasn't about life on the moon. "It's a pleasure to see ya again, Mr. Larkin. I was in the vicinity and thought I'd stop by to see how y'u're enjoying this little town of ours. What have ya seen of it then?"

"Everything in walking distance and Little Chute. What do you recommend I see? You must know this town and the people here better than anyone else around." Maybe a little flattery would throw this reporter off the scent.

"I can recommend a few landmarks if you haven't seen them yet. There's the Hearthstone House, the John Hart Whorton House, and the Zion Lutheran Church. You might want to wander down to the woolen mills or the paper plants at quitting time and watch the people. I used to like to look at their expressions and try to guess what was on their minds. Have you been to Kaukauna then?"

"Not yet."

"Ya know, if ya get your job I still want to do a story about ya, somethin' like boy from the southern coal mines makes good, finds academic career at Lawrence. Do ya have any interestin' story leads for me? Have ya been in touch with your aunt? I'm still trying to locate her."

"The only time I ever I saw her was at my dad's funeral. We talked about my father, made some small talk. I think she used to write to him but never to me." Eryk's ploy didn't work. Didn't Beveridge have an infantry reunion to cover?

"Do ya know her name and address then?"

"Not a clue I'm afraid."

"Care to have dinner with me later, my treat, or did ya have plans to meet someone else?"

"No plans but I'd rather not go out in this weather."

"As ya wish, it was nice talking to you. I still expect an interview when ya get the job if not before."

"Maybe if they make me an offer we'll talk."

* * *

"It seems like a month since I saw you last though it's only been three days," Eryk/Ian said to Vera. "It was hard to wait."

"I couldn't wait to see you again, either. I missed ya."

Neither one of them could keep from looking at the other one.

"Break it up you two," Lyell interjected. "We're here ta study unless ya intend to turn all of us into delinquents."

It was 10:00 AM. They met at the music building to the strains of someone, probably faculty members Robert Adams-Buell and Mrs. Albee, playing Elgar's "Salut d'amour" for piano and violin. From there they walked to the Lawrence College Main Hall to look for a free room.

It was a crisp, pleasant weekend, clear and in the low to midsixties; the weather was begging them to get outdoors and enjoy themselves. Shortly after twelve o'clock they ventured out to find a choice spot on the campus overlooking the river for a picnic. Vera had brought some sliced ham, biscuits, and pears.

"Lyell has big news. Tell him."

"I made the football team!"

"That's great Lyell," Eryk/Ian responded. "What position?"

"I'm a sub on the first team and right end on the scrub team."

"When's your first game?"

"Saturday the 12th. We play Kaukauna. The varsity plays Northwestern."

"I told ya both of my brothers are good," Vera said.

"I'm looking forward to seeing you play, Lyell," Eryk/Ian responded.

"That's right, ya better show up or else," Vera commanded.

"I'll come to see both of you. I'm sure Lyell will be an inspiration and a credit to the team."

"We have ta leave," Lyell said. "We promised ma we'd help 'er this afternoon."

"Goodbye to both of you then. Say hello to your mother for me."

As they walked away Lyell asked Vera, "I thought ya didn't want a boyfriend. Looks to me like y'u're getting' awful attached."

"I'm not so sure any more. There's something different about 'im and he reminds me of father."

* * *

On Saturday the twenty-first Edna Ferber was back in town. She stopped by the Crescent to compare notes with Beveridge.

"Did ya find out anything?" she asked him. "He never went to 'The Store'."

"Some. He keeps to himself. The only friends he's made are a waitress at Griffin's and a woman at the college. Otherwise, he just exchanges pleasantries with some of the people he meets. None of 'em have any information. He's a very tight-lipped fella."

"There's more here than meets the eye. You'd think he'd be asking everyone he meets about Appleton and Lawrence. I think there's something he isn't telling us that he doesn't want to talk about."

"Maybe he's just had a tough life."

"Why do ya say that?"

"I finally managed to talk to both a teacher at his college and his high school principal. Both his parents died tragically and he doesn't have any relatives they know of in Kentucky. The principal said he thought there was an aunt in New York City but I couldn't get a name. With a last name like Larkin there's nothing to go on. He has a few painful memories f'r sure."

"What else you find out?"

"He was the star pupil in his high school. Devoured every book he could get his hands on, just like you. He did tutor and substitute at Cecilian. Then after a while he started applying f'r teaching positions. His teacher said he thought he had five or six interviews lined up around the country and offered to be a reference. Nobody else there expects to hear from him again, but I put the word out that if anyone heard anything, please let me know."

"I'm not so sure this is the same Ian Larkin. He has very little trace of a southern accent or even a Welch accent, and I spent seven years around Welch miners growin' up so I should know. He sounds more Irish than anything else. I'm sure he's not from Kentucky and his parents aren't Welch."

"Something strange might have happened at the train station when he arrived but I don't have any corroboration and I can't be sure. You think maybe he robbed and murdered the real Ian Larkin and took his identity then? Or the two of them have a con or a conspiracy going. That'd be a juicy story, 'n so?"

"That's a possibility."

"But then, why didn't he just disappear into the Western states like all the other criminals? It's clear he's well-educated and he knows his history. That's not the background of your typical killer. It'd be a most unusual set of circumstances. Maybe he has a criminal past and he murdered Larkin and pretends to be him ta hide from his other crimes because it was a good fit."

"The plot just gets thicker, ain'a? There haven't been any murders around here outside of M'waukee, in fact there hasn't been a murder in Appleton the whole time I've lived in Wisconsin. I think he's some sort of grifter and I can't wait to write this story."

"What do ya mean you're writin' the story? This is an Appleton exclusive. Shouldn't ya be sticking to the M'waukee news?"

"We can both write it, you here and me in M'waukee. Nothing fits. So, where's the body?"

"No reports. Prob'ly in some Kentucky coal mine. If he's not the real Larkin, who can we get ta finger him?"

"We need ta solve this puzzle. There's a great story here. I know it; we both know it. Somethin' is very wrong but I can't get my hands on it. I'm sure, he knew me and he knew this town before he even got here. Who would ever hear about a twenty-two-year-old kid reporter in a faraway small town from where he lived? Nobody. Ya know, he *has* ta know someone with a connection ta Appleton. That's where he's getting his information. We need ta crack his cover and find out who his contact is and what they're up to. There's something they he doesn't want us ta know."

"That's a good theory and I'm inclined to believe ya, but it doesn't even explain him. Y'ur tellin' me he's from a small mining town with a hard life and he doesn't even drink like a horse? In fact, he doesn't drink at all? He has a broad sophisticated perspective but he's never left the mining country before? He must've been in New York or Chicago or some big city."

"We need ta get hold of a few hard facts ta confront him with.

Then he'll crack."

"I expect a front-page feature article when I get to the bottom of this. Papers all over the country will pick up on this story."

Chapter Nine
A Healthy Day

Days clicked by.

Sunday the 22nd was a family day for Vera and Lyell. It was clear and in the low sixties, not a day to be indoors, so Eryk/Ian resumed his historical investigation and set out to take a look at the J. B. Courtney Woolen Mills and the Vulcan Street Plant as Beveridge had suggested, but without the comings and goings of the workers. Along the way he saw an ad posted for Professor Sidewinder's Medicine Show. It was on its way to Neenah and would arrive there on Thursday! He determined to go see it.

Monday added rain to the mix. The Hortonville Fair was Monday through Wednesday but the weather wasn't suitable to go. Eryk/Ian stopped at Wollman's and then spent most of the day indoors with his books and magazines. The Crescent published "That Man from New York," one of Eryk/Ian's piano pieces for the day.

On Tuesday Victor Herbert's "Toyland" was on stage at the Appleton Theatre. Eryk especially liked the music and wasn't about to miss it. It was brisk, in the mid-fifties and clear, a good enough day to check out the Hortonville Fair before the show, so he headed for the interurban in the morning.

In the day's news, music publishers were slashing prices because of more efficient printing presses and methods. They announced that sheet music would soon drop to a penny. The State of Milwaukee Bakers announced that either bread would go up from 5 to 6 cents a loaf, or else the loaves would become smaller. The Supreme Court ruled for Appleton in a water rate case but appeals would nevertheless continue.

Naturally, Eryk/Ian's piano practice for the evening included Victor Herbert's "Toyland."

Wednesday finally arrived, a near carbon copy of Tuesday. Meetings with Vera were becoming Eryk's main obsession and this was homework day. Historical investigation was turning into an alsoran. Vera and Lyell would first attend Dr. Plantz's afternoon prayer meeting. In the late 1800s and early 1900s many colleges considered the inculcation of moral values to be of equal importance with academic achievement. Dr. Plantz and Lawrence University seemed to be one of them.

Eryk brought sandwiches Maggie Griffin kindly agreed to make for him along with some apples, pears, and the obligatory cheese, so after homework during the hour before dusk they went to their favorite spot overlooking the river to eat.

"I look forward to our Wednesdays together," Eryk/Ian said. "It's something special for me."

They sat right up next to each other. She started to feed him a sandwich. "Me, too. I can't control myself with ya. Y'u'd better eat this and not say another word." She pushed the sandwich in his mouth as fast as he could chew to make sure.

"I can tell you mean business," he finally said when after his last bite.

After they ate, the three of them went to the Adams-Buell faculty piano recital. It featured a lengthy and ambitious program of Beethoven, Liszt, Mozart, Schubert, Grieg, and others.

Soon, at the conclusion of the concert, it was time for all of them to go home.

"It feels so right when we're together," Vera said. "Say you'll always be my friend and you'll never desert me."

How could he respond? He badly wanted to be with her but the time machine could yank him back any time; events would conspire to keep them apart. "You are very special to me," he said. "I will always care about you and be your friend no matter what the world throws at us. You are the best thing ever. Even if I can't teach at Lawrence and I have to go somewhere else, you are what I will always remember about this place." He watched sadly as the two of them walked away. Maybe there was some way he could return again, and at a point in time when she would never even realize he had gone.

* * *

Thursday was a good day for a medicine show, clear and a rather chilly 60 but suitable enough.

Medicine shows were a tradition that flourished since the late 18th century. Hundreds of them crisscrossed the country. They ranged from simple mom-and-pop operations to elaborate shows sponsored by large manufacturers. In fact, some manufacturers sent a dozen or more shows to tour the country and sell their products.

People were susceptible to these shows. They feared diseases like cataleptic neuroplexy and the vapors, and actively sought remedies. At the turn of the twentieth century, physicians were scarce and poorly educated. Most treatments were based on the supposed four bodily humors that had to be kept in balance. Unfortunately, the treatments that were devised to restore this balance could definitely be worse than the disease. As a result, people clamored for patent medicines, whether from a traveling show, the local druggist, or from a mail order catalog.

The shows used entertainment to attract an audience, and as a matrix to deliver the sales pitch. Integral to the show were stories, stories that served to both entertain and deliver enticing anecdotes about miraculous drugs being magnanimously offered to the audience for a mere pittance. Clearly, aficionados of medicine shows would be right at home watching modern TV.

Vaudeville style acts and stories might comprise forty to fifty per cent of a typical show. The showman extolled the product (or several), delivering his finely honed sales pitch for another forty per cent or more of the time. The remaining 10% or so was the actual selling, collecting money in exchange for the goods. When the selling dried up the show was over, and sometimes very suddenly at that.

The showman typically called himself "Professor" or "Doctor", and he always had an exclusive connection with a genius with the forbidden knowledge, the one who made the once in a thousand-year discovery, the one who unearthed the ancient secret, the enlightened one who solved the ancient mysteries, or the Indian medicine man who carefully guarded his secrets but agreed to share them with the showman.

The salesman was an expert at working the crowd, sensing their frame of mind and pacing the show in order to build excitement and momentum, manipulating them right to the very end. He would entice, coerce, shame, trick, or harass them and use every other means at his disposal to motivate them into buying his products, wherever his skilled reading of the crowd led. He had an eye for spotting skeptics in the audience and cajoling them.

The entertainment would gradually build up to some grand stunt. The showman knew how to build excitement and anticipation until the crowd became restless and longed to get their hands on the product. And he promised them something they desperately wanted to believe in. The claims became increasingly bolder and extravagant as the show progressed. As soon as the showman sensed the crowd couldn't stand any more, the selling began, sometimes in midperformance. A good showman built up a group psychology, a herd mentality, so that as soon as one person started to buy, they all followed at once like sheep. As soon as all the remedies were sold that could be, the showman would quickly fold up shop and vanish as rapidly as he could.

The medicines were typically alcohol laden formulas sold during intermission and after the show. Snake oils were a special favorite because they were commonly believed to have potent medicinal powers. Wizard oil, cough balsam, blood liver pills, and swamp root were also in high demand. Besides copious amounts of alcohol, some remedies contained opiates or cocaine, so the customers felt good at first and then lapsed into habitual use.

Interestingly, a rare few of the cures sold at medicine shows actually did have merit and are still around under the same or new names. For example, Vick's VapoRub, originally Richardson's Croup and Pneumonia Cure Salve, Milk of Magnesia, Listerine, Ex-Lax, and Bayer Aspirin, as well as some herbal remedies originally sold at medicine shows, can be effective and are still sold.

Alas, most of the elixirs and remedies didn't work at best or were fraudulent or even harmful at worst, and people quickly became wise to the trickery. Once a certain territory was worked over, or "burnt up" in carnie jargon, no medicine show could or would return until memories faded.

And now, here it was! They were setting up the stage. Maybe it was six feet by nine feet. This was one of the smaller one-wagon shows, so it was a quick set-up.

A man, maybe in his mid-twenties, in a brown vested suit and red four-hand tie came out with a chair and a banjo. He set the chair on the left front corner of the stage, placed the banjo on the chair, and moved to the center of the small stage. He took some large pins out of a box that was intentionally left there and started juggling them, three, four, five, and finally an astounding six pins at once! Then he put the pins back in the box, went to the chair, took the banjo, and sat down. He started to strum his instrument. After a few minutes he began to sing a mix of old familiar songs, Stephen Foster songs and new tunes like "Bye Bye Birdie", "Harrigan", "Tipperary", and "Budweiser's a Friend of Mine".

As people started to gather around, a woman in a modest wraparound hat with a big plume, dressed in a long-pleated gold dress with huge padded shoulders, came out with a flea circus in a large glass box she set up on a table in the center of the stage. The box was perhaps a foot by a foot and a half. The fleas jumped around and seemed to do tricks, jumping through hoops, on and off a high wire, chasing each other, but it all happened so fast who could tell? Some of the fleas were controlled by very fine, nearly invisible gold wires. Some shows used electro-magnets. They all counted on fast action and tiny fleas to give an illusion that the fleas were trained to do tricks.

Eryk/Ian found a spot off to the side where he hoped he wouldn't be noticed.

When the crowd numbered maybe forty adults plus assorted children, a well-dressed fortyish man in a bulky three-piece grey suit with large wide lapels, light blue shirt, a thick golden tie, and a tall black hat with a grey band strode onto the stage and started his spiel, just as the flea circus woman folded up her act.

"By a set of fortuitous circumstances, you are all privileged to learn about an elixir, a new and one-of-a-kind secret formula that will make you healthy, disease free and youthful beyond your dreams. Come close and see for yourself. You will be amazed. Do you want to see your health perfected and your youthful vigor restored? Of course you do! Who can pass up this opportunity? Who would be so foolish they would turn a deaf ear? Nobody, not you, not your neighbors, not your friends. Everyone who discovers this secret must have it, they must have the elixir. I will tell you frankly my friends and countrymen, the supply of this superior formula is limited. There isn't enough to go around. The smartest among you will get theirs now while they still can! Just stick around, you will be glad you did!"

Did the showman know full well his magic elixir was a fraud but was nevertheless possessed by a cynical, greedy determination to take the money of every sucker he could find, or did he somehow delude himself that his concoction was actually therapeutic?

When this first commercial finally ended the flea lady had transformed herself. She now appeared onstage in a shirtwaist, short skirt, and tights. It turned out she was also a contortionist. The banjo man stood and played while she painfully twisted and folded herself into pretzel shapes. After a few minutes the showman started explaining how this woman had once been stiff as a board, but after a year of consuming the elixir, her joints and indeed, her entire body, returned to its former state of youthful flexibility. This spiel was followed by a selection of corny jokes from banjo-man.

The showman continued his story. "My elixir is an old Shawnee medicine, refined over many generations by a succession of medicine men who passed the knowledge of the secret ingredients down over the years. At 149 years old, the last of these in the line, Chief Red Tree, didn't know what to do about his medicine. He was fearful it would no longer be consumed wisely. His way of life was vanishing with his people, so who was left to still benefit from it? Where was the next medicine man to experience this knowledge? There wasn't one. How could Chief Red Tree preserve the secret for future Indian generations? He told me it was better if his medicine was used by the wise deserving few wherever they came from. Would I help him? I gladly took up the challenge."

A man in the middle of the crowd was shuffling and smiling. He seemed to be laughing to himself. "You in the plaid shirt, you seem skeptical. You want be the only one who is too cheap to improve your health? Will you be the only one here to go home without this curative elixir? Cast your doubts aside and wait, I will show you the immense benefits of this one-of-a-kind formula."

Banjo-man came out again to continue his musical entertainment, this time with an accordion. This being Wisconsin, he started playing a set of polkas. Just as he was building a head of steam, the multi-talented flea woman rejoined him with a dance, a snake dance, with a live, barely controlled five-foot venomouslooking snake. Eryk/Ian didn't know what kind of snake it was, but he was glad he wasn't in the front row.

"How can I offer you this exclusive, one-of-a-kind formula? This formula will be the smartest purchase you ever made. I've scoured the country for the exact ingredients, nature's very own herbs and plants, all of them rare and hard to find, finally gathering them for your edification as I will soon demonstrate. The Chief's own secret formula. This exclusive formula will cure rheumatism, cancer, diabetes, bad breath, curvature of the spine, senility, consumption, effluvia, French pox, digestive problems, chill fever, female hysteria, cholera, nervous prostration, and female complaints. It will succeed where all of the doctors have failed. How much is that worth? Well my friends, half a dollar is all it takes to have your own bottle of the Chief's medicine, a mere half a dollar to put a bounce in your step, add radiance to your face, watch your ailments recede, and feel your strength building. Step up, get your bottle while they last, enjoy the unique benefits of this elixir while it is still available. Do it now." The selling commenced.

Eryk knew that the 1906 Pure Food and Drug Act marked the slow, gradual decline of the medicine show. It had now passed its peak as a form of entertainment.

* * *

Friday the 27th was Lyell's birthday, a family affair for the Bleeckers. Eryk/Ian went to the phone company office to phone him and wish him a happy birthday. It was also the last day of the Seymour Fair, clear and cold with temperatures in the low fifties, barely decent enough for a fair, but Eryk/Ian decided he had seen enough horse races, commercial booths, carnival games, carnival food, vaudeville acts, baking contests, and animal judging that week. Vera and Eryk/Ian had plans to go to Lake Winnebago on Saturday, but it was in the mid-fifties with occasional rain. They met for supper at

Griffin's instead. A double feature of musicals, "Teddy and His Bear" and "Iolanthe," were playing at the Appleton Theatre.
Maybe she would like to see them.

"Ian," she said in a rehearsed tone of voice, "I'm sorry but I'm becoming too attached to you. What if ya don't get the job at Lawrence and ya have to leave me? I mean, I think you should get it, but what if ya don't? When my father died, I was just a little girl but I thought I would never recover from it. I was so sad for so long. Then my brothers went off to boarding school and left me alone. The men in my life keep leaving me and I don't think I can handle another disappointment. Can ya understand it?"

"Yes, I understand. You know I've thought about it myself," Eryk/Ian replied lamely. "It's hard for me but maybe it's for the best."

"I have tah go now. Good luck. Call me if ya get the job and ya wanna make a commitment."

"You can be sure I will. I'll miss you, Vera. I'll miss you a lot."

Eryk would be dining alone that evening.

Chapter Ten
The Game

Time passed slowly after Vera's departure. Eryk's interest in how it actually felt to live in historic times evaporated. The days became all alike.

Sunday dawned clear with temperatures rising from the forties toward the low sixties. It was a nice enough day but Eryk/Ian didn't feel like doing much. He finally pushed himself to choose a book and walk to City Park to try to read it. Maybe he would see Vera there, after all, it wasn't far from her house. Of course, she wasn't there. He wasn't up to practicing songs on the piano that evening.

Monday dawned clear and a little colder than the day before. Eryk/Ian picked at his breakfast of cream toast and fruit, stewed chicken slices, fried potatoes, sliced tomatoes, and coffee. As a consolation he went to Lake Winnebago alone despite the chill. At least there were no memories of being there with Vera, so he could concentrate on taking care of himself and snapping out of his funk.

His musical selection that evening was a sad but heart-felt rendition of Chopin's Waltz in A-flat major ("Farewell").

The rest of the week featured temperatures in the low sixties and seventies along with an occasional drizzle except for Wednesday's steady rain.

That Tuesday the first was Ian's interview. Eryk/Ian couldn't bring himself to intentionally blow it and he decided to give it his best shot. He was interviewed by Carl Christophelsmeier of the history department, May Esther Carter, associate professor of literature and dean of women, and Emma Kate Corkhill on English literature. He had to wait a week or two for their decision until they finished interviewing all of the candidates.

There was a dance that night at Harmonie Hall sponsored by the Caroline Lodge. There was also a basso song recital by Lawrence faculty member William Harper at the Methodist church. Eryk/Ian chose to go to the latter. He hoped to see Vera somewhere on the campus. It was a mistake. He never got a glimpse and everywhere he went reminded him of her.

When Eryk/Ian returned to the boarding house he made a halfhearted attempt at playing "Let's Play Keeping House" which was published in the Crescent that evening. It was probably the worst rendition in Appleton that evening.

The week dragged on. Eryk kept reminding himself it was his last chance to experience the times for what they were, an opportunity no other historian had ever had. He told himself to shape up and focus on his mission before it was too late.

On Wednesday afternoon, after a dinner consisting of boiled beef with potatoes, turnips, pickled beets, apple pie, pears, carrot cake, walnuts, and coffee, Eryk/Ian popped open his umbrella and headed for the Bijou. The performers that day included the Kinsners' balancing act (for example, balancing anvils on their chin), the Kimball Brothers' comedy act, soprano Inez Montague, and contortionist London Blunt, as well as the usual kinescope movies.

That evening, following the afternoon show, Eryk/Ian again went to Griffins for supper. Before he could take a seat Karen intercepted him. "Such a long face," she said. "What's the matter?"

"You needn't worry about me. I'll be fine."

"Ya haven't been here with your Gibson girl Miss Vera for a while, is that the reason for the sad look?"

"Maybe. What's the remedy?"

"How about a slice of chocolate cake? Maggie has a new recipe. Chocolate is highly medicinal ya know."

"So I've heard. Why don't you bring me the whole cake?"

"Then what do I tell my other customers? I'll bring ya a slice and ya can see if that's enough, ain'a?"

"You should have been a doctor."

"Then I'd have to give ya a bill."

In sports news the Phillies' Eddie Grant went 7 for 7 in a double header against the Giants. Consequently, Eryk/Ian attempted "Take me out to the Ballgame" for his practice that night.

Thursday was a good day to catch the Oneida Fair at Du Pere. Temperatures were in the upper sixties with just a few sprinkles every now and then, enough to keep the crowds down but not enough to discourage Eryk/Ian from going. The fair advertised itself as the only Indian fair in the country, with horse races, baseball, lacrosse, various vaudeville acts, and the usual vendors and judging events, so it was something a little different. Maybe there would be a few Indians and some different kinds of people at this one.

Friday was just like Thursday but a few degrees cooler. Eryk perked up when he learned that Pearson's Music was having a piano sale. Prices ranged from $187.50 to $262.50. He went to have a look and try out the merchandise. It was enough of a distraction to get him back to studying people's habits and beliefs and how they lived, and to a closer examination of the day's events.

The news of the day was a runaway train engine pulling five cars that crashed into the Saecker warehouse, knocking a large hole in the side of the building and causing considerable damage to both the train and the warehouse. The accident was caused by a damaged rail. No one was injured.

In other news of vital importance, Gladys Vanderbilt, the youngest Vanderbilt child, announced her engagement to Count Laszio Szechenyi of Budapest. It was the desire of affluent American families of the day to validate themselves by seeking to marry off a daughter or two to the European nobility. Another article bemoaned that bicycles on the sidewalk were running down more pedestrians but the police were powerless to do anything about it. Eryk/Ian also learned that lumberjacks were in greater demand, commanding pay of $35 a month plus room and board.

For that evening's practice Eryk/Ian played "The Cakewalk" by Arthur Sullivan, published in the Crescent that day.

Ian would have been nervous waiting for a decision about the instructor position. Eryk of course knew the outcome in advance, so he was merely indifferent.

Saturday was like Friday without the drizzle. Eryk/Ian wanted to find a Wild West show to see somewhere. There were dozens of them traveling the country, but none nearby so he decided to take the short and inter-urban, which ran hourly, past Little Chute to Kaukauna with its paper, limber, and flour mills, so he could walk around and explore the place. It was a small town bisected by the Fox River.

In sports news that day, Philadelphia's Rube Vickers no-hit Washington Senators 4-0 in five innings.

On Sunday there was a German comedy at St. Joseph's Hall. Maybe the Saeckers would be there but Eryk/Ian didn't go to find out. It was fine weather, so instead he paid a visit to some of the landmark buildings Beveridge recommended.

The Palace Theater began a six-day blockbuster run of "The Life of Christ" on Monday. Eryk/Ian didn't go but opted to continue his research at the public library on Oneida Street. There were plenty of books, magazines, and memoirs that wouldn't exist in another hundred years. The day was clear and crisp so he decided to walk there and take the long way around. He knew better than to pass by the Bleecker house along the way, but somehow his feet never got the message. He didn't see anyone and just grew sadder.

For dinner back at the boarding house Mrs. Bowe served roast beef, potatoes, eggplant, succotash, watermelon, carrot cake, Wisconsin cheese, sugar wafers from the H. W. Grainger bakery, and coffee. There was a new boarder, a thin gaunt coughing man in a dark gray suit from Madison who replaced the two students. He was newly employed by one of the paper mills.

Maybe Eryk/Ian should have gone to Griffin's instead. No sooner had he started to walk down Appleton Street towards Oneida on his way back to the library than Beveridge accosted him. "Hello, Mr. Larkin. I heard ya had y'ur interview last Tuesday. How'd it go then?"

"I think it went well. I worked hard to prepare for it."

"Are ya still enjoying your stay here in Appleton?"

Eryk/Ian answered truthfully, "It's not like the place I grew up in. I'm learning a lot here."

"Good, good. Ya know, I located y'ur aunt in New York. I'm tryin' to arrange a telephone interview with 'er. Is there anything ya want to tell me first while I'm preparing to talk to 'er?"

"Not really. I didn't have any contact with her you know except at the funeral. Anyway, if I don't get the job, you won't have anything to write about."

"Y'u're still a good story either way. Why don't ya give me an interview before I talk to y'ur aunt? Provide me with some background. It will help me find a focus for my story."

"There is no doubt in my mind your readers will yawn and fall asleep. There are a thousand stories in this town more interesting than mine."

"Ya may be right but I have to follow my journalistic instincts."

It was a good thing the polygraph hadn't been invented yet.

* * *

This was an historic occasion. The first of only three tie games in World Series history. It would end with a score of 2-2. There would probably never again be another tie since modern stadiums all have floodlights. There was no World Series game in Ian Larkin's journal, but how could he possibly miss this? He would never in his entire life forgive himself. He bought a round trip to Chicago on the Chicago and Northwestern for the early morning departure. He wanted to make sure he had plenty of time to find his way once he got to the station.

Skies were clear and it was in the mid-fifties, a good fall baseball day. Upon arriving at the ticket window Eryk bought a 50cent ticket (twice the regular season price) for one of the cheap seats along the right outfield. He could have afforded better, but there was a crush of people and he wanted to sit in the most inconspicuous spot he could with little chance of a foul ball flying in his direction.

Eryk was way early but he found his seat and settled in to wait and enjoy the game. This was special, not like any other game he had ever seen. The fact that he knew exactly what would happen felt strange, special, unique, and weird all at once. Nevertheless, he could hardly contain himself seeing baseball as it was once played in an original late nineteenth century stadium by legends the likes of Ty Cobb and Tinker-Evers-Chance.

He looked around while he waited, enthusiastically soaking up every dimension of the experience he could. The West Side Park was a wooden stadium; there were 24,337 fans that day overflowing the park in a stadium built for 16,000. Many of them were allowed to stand in the playing field along the grandstand walls. The park had a high covered double deck behind the plate at the outside center of which was a small brick structure topped with player statues, housing the ticket and team offices. The double deck extended beyond third base to just past the 340-foot foul line in left field, where it gave way to uncovered bleachers. Similarly, on the right side the double deck continued just past the 340-foot right field foul line where it gave way to much narrower uncovered bleachers only five to ten rows deep with billboards behind. Dead center field was 560 feet. The park was not symmetrical, since left field was notably deeper and more spacious than right field.

Finally, at 3:30, the Cubs' Orval Overall hurled the first pitch and the historic game was underway. Eryk/Ian settled in.

By the top of the eighth the Cubs led one to nothing, but that was about to change. With one out, Tigers left fielder Davy Jones singled and stole second. Second baseman Schaefer then grounded to third but reached on an error, with Jones advancing to third. Center fielder "Wahoo Sam" Crawford then singled in both Jones and Schaefer. He advanced to third on an error by the catcher. The Tigers now led 2 to 1. The infamous Ty Cobb then grounded to the pitcher who threw to the shortstop Joe Tinker covering third to get Crawford who was off the bag, but Tinker dropped the ball for the third error of the inning. Cobb took advantage to run to second. Crawford returned to third leaving runners at second and third with one away. Eryk knew, however, that the Tigers' threat was about to be snuffed out.

The next batter, first baseman Claude Rossman, flied to shallow center with Crawford tagging. He wouldn't beat the throw home to Cubs catcher Johnny Kling. Or would he? Kling dropped the ball on the collision at the plate! This was not supposed to happen! It was 3 to 1. A 2-2 tie was now impossible! Instead of leading off the ninth, third baseman Bill Coughlin came to bat and struck out to end the top half of the inning.

Eryk didn't know what to expect next.

The Cubs were out 1-2-3 in the bottom half of the eighth.

The Tigers first batter in the ninth reached on still another Chicago error, but the next three batters made outs, leaving him stranded.

Now it was the bottom of the ninth. The Cubs seemed determined to blow the game with their five errors and twelve strikeouts, and they were down to their last three outs. First baseman and team manager Frank Chance led off with a single to right field. Third baseman Harry Steinfeldt was hit by a pitch. Kling then blew an attempted sacrifice bunt, popping out to first. Next, second baseman

Johnny Evers reached on a Tigers shortstop error, leaving the bases loaded with one out. Right fielder Frank Schulte next grounded out first baseman to pitcher covering for the second out, scoring Chance and leaving the other two runners in scoring position with two out. Del Howard, batting for Tinker, struck out.

Eryk knew that should have ended the game with a Tiger win, but this time Detroit catcher Boss Schmidt muffed the pitch on the third strike! Howard took off for first. Steinfeldt scored on the catcher's throw to first which was too late to get the third out and end the game. Meanwhile, Evers advanced to third. Pat Moran came up to pinch hit for Cubs pitcher Orval Overall. During Moran's at-bat Moran stole second, but it didn't matter. Evers was thrown out attempting to steal home, ending the inning.

The game continued three more innings with no runs scored by either side. It was called on account of darkness since there were no stadium floodlights, ending in a 3-3 tie.

"Oh crap," Eryk said to himself. He realized something he did or said changed history! Would someone's life change forever for the worse because of what he had done? Would anyone die or never be born because of him? Eryk was overcome with guilt. He couldn't sit still. He needed to do something to right the situation, but what? Who had he talked to that day and what had he said? Who did he bump into or disturb? Was it something he did or said on a previous day that, by some random chain of events, made its way to the game? Eryk went over and over the past several days' events, trying to figure out what went wrong and what he might do about it.

For right now, all he could do was to hurry back to his room and hunker down there, doing nothing unless he thought of a way to fix this glitch, and wait for the exchange back, lest he make things even worse.

Chapter Eleven
Life Goes On

Life went on as usual in Appleton, without Eryk/Ian's participation. The weather continued fair, 60 to 70 degrees each day but windy on Thursday. Wednesday was the Eagles' annual dance at the Armory. Plays continued at the Appleton Theatre as did Lawrence faculty violin recitals at the Methodist Church.

An ad in the Crescent posted positions for draftsmen at $75 to $250 a month depending on experience. The Daily Post noted that teachers were in demand in the west, with starting salaries of forty to fifty dollars a month for new teachers in the Dakotas where room and board could be had for two to three dollars a week. Fifty dollars a month was a typical salary at the time, although budgetary records for the Chicago area show that high ranking public officials could make as much as $350 or more, all tax free. There were no income or payroll taxes yet.

The price of a shave at union barber shops was about to increase to fifteen cents. It looked like Eryk was leaving town just in time.

Friday's musical revue at the Appleton Theater, "The Girl over There," featured a "diamond chorus of beautiful girls." It opened to good reviews and a packed audience. Eryk/Ian was not among them.

Eryk quietly and listlessly made his observations and followed current events.

But then, Friday evening, Eryk/Ian received an unexpected visit from Lyell.

"Ian, my sister isn't herself lately. No spark at all. I'm starting on the scrub team against Kaukauna tomorrow. Will ya come tah watch?"

"Sure, I wanted to see a game before I left anyway. What about Vera?"

"She'll be there but she won't be expecting to see *you*. I'll tell in the morning I invited ya. Look for her."

"I'll listen for the explosion."

"Ya know where the Lawrence athletic field is don't ya?"

"On the line to Kaukauna."

"Don't forget. If the two of yous can straighten things out it will be better for both of ya."

"I'll do my best."

"Thanks. I'll look for both of yous after the game."

Eryk got to the field early to try to spot Vera on her way to the bleachers. He decided that if she shied away from him, it would be best he just sat in a different area and went his own way afterwards. She saw him standing near the entrance and went directly over.

"Vera, I've missed you so much. You're all I think about."

"It's the same for me."

"You were right. I didn't get the job. I have to leave for St. Louis in a few days. A college near there is interviewing me for a position they have."

"I know. I'm first in line for the school gossip, remember? Will ya write me?"

"Yes. I'll find a way to see you again." It was a promise Eryk wanted to keep but likely never could. Even if he found a way it would be dangerous, but he ached to see Vera, to somehow be with her one day.

"Please don't forget me."

"Never."

Next thing Eryk knew she kissed him and he kissed her back. He drew it out as long as he could, precious seconds until she finally withdrew.

Lawrence won the game by a touchdown, 5-0. Afterwards the three of them hooked up near the locker room.

They took the trolley back from the field, reliving the game in their conversation the entire time. Vera and Lyell got off at the Lawe Street stop. She looked at him and said simply, "Goodbye, love." With that she turned to leave. Eryk watched her in agony as she disappeared from his life, most likely forever.

There was a dramatic reading at the Appleton Theatre that evening. Maybe it would take Eryk's mind off Vera, or maybe he should just walk around town and take everything in one last time.

He ended up wandering around town until dusk. He didn't feel much like supper. For his evening practice he chose a rather nostalgic rendering of Stephen Foster's "Beautiful Dreamer."

Then he knew he had to start preparing for his departure.

* * *

The next afternoon Ferber cornered Eryk/Ian in his room. Pouring on her charm hadn't worked and time was up. She decided on a new tack.

"You and I both know there's a story here and I won't leave without it. Ya may as well tell me what y'u're really doing here. We both know ya aren't from Kentucky and I don't think y'u're Ian Larkin, either. Too many things don't fit.

"I gotta tell ya Byron contacted Ian Larkin's aunt in New York City. She said Ian Larkin is asthmatic, a light smoker, and he drank a few shots of whiskey at his father's funeral. Nobody has seen ya wheezing or drinking. Ya recognized me when you first saw me. Why don't ya confide in me before someone else discovers your secret, someone less sympathetic?"

Eryk didn't know how to get this dog off the scent but he had to do something and carefully, very carefully. He had to get her to leave his room and he didn't want to trigger her notorious temper in the process. She would have to leave to catch the late train to

Milwaukee eventually but by then it would be too late. Or would she wait until the next morning to return?

"I've told you my story and I don't know what else to say," he said as gently as he could manage. "I know you and Mr. Beveridge are checking up on me and I know you are both very professional in your work. My aunt doesn't know me and I'm sure everything else you've found out confirms my story. You have to realize by now I'm a very private man and that won't change."

"Then can ya convince me that y'u're the real Ian Larkin? We'd both like to confirm y'ur story. There's a few discrepancies starting when you arrived at the train station."

"If you've contacted my friends and teachers back in Henderson you have your proof." At least that's what Eryk hoped, but if either of them ever did manage to arrange a phone call with someone or go to Kentucky who knew Larkin well enough, there was no telling what they would find out. Maybe she would call Beveridge to play good cop-bad cop with him. Too bad for her they didn't have cell phones.

"Tell me more. I'll keep ya company here as long as I can. We can talk history. It's one of the few subjects I had a knack for in school. She intended a history interrogation, too, to see if he would slip and reveal something he shouldn't know, knowledge about a place he'd been to or someone he'd talked to but wouldn't acknowledge.

It was time for the exchange. So Eryk didn't bite and refused to leave his room. He had no choice but to stay. The exchange must occur or history would be shattered. What would happen if Ferber saw the exchange happen, right before her eyes? Was there any way out? It was too late to lock the door and refuse to let her in. The consequences were now unknowable. Eryk's mind drifted off. There was nothing more he could do. Ferber's persistent questions, her insistent, angry tone didn't penetrate. Eryk stood quiet and waited. He waited some more. Nothing happened.

Chapter Twelve
Antiques

"It's perfect," Trice announced. "The plans are finished. We'll have the building ready in three months."

As a spy agency, the National Intelligence Administration could do as it pleased with its more than ample secret budget. It was not bothered with building permits and inspections, historical preservation or environmental regulations and studies, competitive bids and proposal evaluations, or any of the other impediments that might delay its urgent, timely, and incredibly important life-or-death mission. It didn't have to reveal any of its classified activities to the public.

Soon the 1900-era mansion would be restored to its original appearance and transformed into the Milwaukee Blue Mound Sanatorium, a private facility for 40 patients that opened in 1907. In it were once treated private patients with mild cases of tuberculosis and other diseases with an "optimistic prognosis," for the outrageous fee of $10 a week.

The building was situated on large, secluded and mostly wooded twenty-three-acre site far from highway noises and other indications of modern times, with only the sound of an occasional jet to shatter the mood.

As soon as Ian Larkin appeared in the time machine's inner chamber he was drugged and brought to the house as patient number three. He didn't bear a close resemblance to Eryk, a bit shorter, rounder face, unshaven, close-fitting brown suit and black tie, but a similar medium build.

Trice's strategy was to keep Larkin in the "sanatorium" under the ruse that he was exposed to consumption, that is, tuberculosis, and he was showing symptoms of the disease. He intended to dull Larkin's senses with drugs so he wouldn't remember anything and he couldn't think to escape. Furthermore, he wasn't to get the slightest glimpse of modern life to take back with him. Trice delegated Heller to assist. Part of her assignment was to talk to Larkin and get as much information about his history and future plans as she could.

Trice introduced himself to Larkin.

"Hello Mr. Larkin. I'm Dr. Ernst, the director of this sanatorium here in Milwaukee. You were brought here as a precaution because you were exposed to consumption. You were wheezing and breathing hard and you fainted. You need to be treated. I expect you to be here for about a month."

"But ah didn't ask tah be brought cheer. Ah don't have the scratch for this place."

"Don't worry, there's no charge. We just opened and we want to establish our reputation. You're one of our very first patients."

"Ah'm jake. Ah want tah leave now." He said wheezing a bit. "Ah have an interview to go to at Lawrence."

"I'm afraid that's not a good idea. There's a chance you might infect others. We need to be sure. There's no need for you to worry. We'll make sure you're back in Appleton in time for your interview. Now I'd like to introduce you to Violet Jensen, our superintendent."

"Hello Mr. Larkin, I'm happy to meet you," Heller said.

"Pleased tah meet yah Miss Jensen."

"We have two other patients right now. You are our third. The names of the other two are Stanley Brinker and Oliver Danbury."

In reality, the other two "patients" were detectives tasked to be sure Larkin remained mildly drugged, satisfied, and captive.

"When you are feeling better, we'd like you to fill out our application form, just to make everything official. One of our nurses will explain the rules and the daily routine to you."

"Bloody hell, ah didn't ask tah be hyeh and ah won't fill out no form."

"As you wish." There was actually no application form. It was just a ruse to make the "sanatorium" seem more realistic.

"Are you feeling better now?" Heller continued.

"Ah'm done in."

"Then why don't you rest. I'm sure you'll find your bed comfortable and your room pleasant. We have good food and a relaxing atmosphere which I'm sure you will find pleasing."

"Yeah, hangin' place ya have hyeh." Larkin was wheezing again.

He dozed off in his bed, one of a dozen lining the walls of a large room along with four stuffed chairs, a small medical table and a small sink. Brinker and Danbury occupied two of the other beds. The large and plentiful row of windows were left open except on the coldest of nights to circulate therapeutic fresh air. There was a double door leading out to the porch that spanned the entire length of the second floor. The walls and ceiling were plain white plaster and the floors were oak planked. Electric light fixtures hung down from the twelve-foot-high ceilings. Additional chairs and beds lined the porch.

"Are you a scientist or a jailer?" Heller teased Trice.

"I don't feel right about this, but it's a practical necessity. We have to keep him lightly sedated so he doesn't learn anything beyond his time and take it back. That would surely destroy us. I'd like to treat his asthma with modern drugs but we don't dare do that, either."

"Do you know what the scariest word in the English language was in 1907? It was 'consumption.' One in every five to seven Americans died from it. Just that one word will keep him in line." "I don't want to scare the poor boy to death."

The Milwaukee Blue Mound Sanatorium featured a fine new building, good air, large beautiful gardens, good food, quiet rest, an exercise gym, baths, massage, indoor plumbing, and electric lights and amenities. Cheerful, sunny rooms and comfortable porches with a view of the gardens were features of the place. It was strictly private, walled off and isolated, with a long tree-lined gravel driveway.

At the dawn of the self-proclaimed "American Century" consumption, that is, tuberculous, was the number one health scourge. Sanatoria were the standard of treatment, although poorer victims of the disease often ended up in private homes, caves, tents, basements, and so-called dispensaries.

From the outside, the building looked like a long dark yellow two-story rectangular inn covered with horizontal wood siding. Wide full-length porches adorned both floors in front of the house, supported by a series of posts and railings. Behind the porches, closely spaced five-foot high windows lined the front of the house except in the center of the first floor where the main entrance doors were located. The high-pitched roof had five dormers front and back with two additional windows at each end. This third-floor roof space housed the rooms and offices of the sanatorium staff. There were four chimneys sticking up above the roof, one at each end and two in the middle.

Most sanatoria were private and affordable only by the upper and upper-middle classes. They relied on the belief that rest, fresh air, good food, and exercise were curative for diseases such as tuberculosis. It was believed that for mild cases of consumption, at least, the body could wall off pockets of the disease in the lungs, containing the disease and leading to a kind of cure.

Beyond that, isolating victims of the disease would prevent them from infecting others. In the 1800s Koch discovered that tuberculosis was caused by an infectious bacterium. Some local governments even shipped victims off to sanatoriums in other states to protect their own populations, which helped result in sanatoria becoming a big business, especially in Colorado, California, Arizona, Texas and some other western states. Indeed, Denver grew quite noticeably from the influx of tuberculosis patients.

New patients generally had to apply for admission and agree to follow the strict rules of the institution. The emphasis was on bedrest in the open air, on sleeping on porches or in well-ventilated rooms. Coughing and spitting in common areas or on the floor was generally prohibited. Patients were expected to control spray from the lungs, throat or mouth. Mild to moderate exercise was stressed, which often included housework and maintenance of the facility. Patients were not to allow themselves to get out of breath, especially if they had a fever or were tired, and they were to avoid overly strenuous exercise. Each patient was urged to play an active part in their own cure. Most establishments emphasized compassionate and very adequate nursing care.

There was great variation in the size, location, and treatment of sanatoria. Some were harsh, with residents sleeping outdoors every night regardless of the weather and with taxing exercise regimens, while others were more like posh resorts. A sanatorium might house anywhere from six to hundreds of patients.

Trice interrupted Larkin as he was waking up.

"Mr. Larkin, I've brought Dr. Whiteman to look at your wheezing and see what we can do for you," he said.

"Hello Mr. Larkin. How long have you had asthma?" Whiteman asked.

"Since ah was twelve."

"Does it run in your family?"

"Ah don't have no fam'ly but some o' the other breaker boys done got it, too."

"I see. How long were you a breaker boy?"

"Three years, summers when ah weren't in school."

"I'd like to listen to your lungs to see if they're congested." It was difficult for Whiteman to accept the fact that he could only use 1900-era medical equipment and protocols. He agreed to it and signed a secrecy oath, but he didn't understand why it was necessary.

"Ah need a drag. Where's mah smokes?"

"I believe they're against the sanatorium rules and smoking will make your asthma much worse. You need to quit so you can breathe better and stop wheezing."

"Ah didn't agree to no rules. Don't be a killjoy. Ah done smoked since ah was a kid."

"I'm afraid I must insist that you stop for the sake of your health. Do you want a patch to help you quit?"

"What do yah mean 'patch?' Ah don't like the sounds o' that."

"Never mind then. Just focus on the good food and exercise regimen here and pay attention to how much easier you'll breathe without your smokes. In a week or two you'll be happy about it."

"Can Ah have whiskey with mah meals?"

"I believe they provide some fine wines with midday and evening meals."

"Better be something Ah like. Ah'm not happy tah be hyeh."

Breaker boys were usually aged 10 to 12 years, too young to be employed as miners. Sometimes old, diseased, or maimed men who were no longer able to work in the mines took up the same dangerous work. Their pay was less than half of a miner's pay. Their job was to separate impurities from coal by hand from coal breakers and conveyer belts. Despite public disapproval, companies employed these workers from the mid-1880s until the 1920s. Since the washed coal was slick, they had to work without gloves. The impurities had sharp edges leading to cut fingers. Sometimes breaker boys lost fingers, hands, feet, or arms because of the rapidly moving belts or because they were caught in belts or gears. Some were even crushed or smothered to death. There was so much blinding coal dust that many boys developed lung diseases. Coal was often washed to remove impurities, creating sulfuric acid that further damaged lungs, hands, and eyes.

"Trice," Whiteman said when he stepped outside the room, "This man has a definite wheeze, asthma, but his nails have a bluish twinge. I suspect pneumoconiosis or emphysema but I need an x-ray to confirm it. He needs an inhaler and probably something for lung obstruction."

"I'd like to say 'OK' but I can't. There were no medical x-rays yet in the early twentieth century. We have to go with the sanatorium treatment."

"I don't understand this insistence on hundred-and-twentyfive-year-old treatments. Is it because this is some mental case you're treating? This man really thinks he was born in 1883. And another thing, there haven't been any breaker boys for a hundred years. Clearly delusional."

"Something like that."

Heller had her own plan and it started with establishing a comfortable daily routine at "Blue Mound," a routine that made everybody complacent and less diligent.

She wanted Larkin to relax and fall into a habitual schedule. Brinker and Danbury were to accompany him at all times except when one of them was called out to be briefed or to catch up on his Facebook. She tasked them with finding out what Larkin liked to eat and what he liked to read while he rested, then it would be provided in an authentic-appearing 1907 version.

The daily routine consisted of meals in the dining hall amidst a lot of empty tables, light exercise in the gym, supervised walks around the garden, and plenty of rest. If boredom set in, she might add use of a rowboat in the large pond and maybe some shuffleboard. Larkin would see the same two "nurses," housekeeper, and waiter every day. Most of the rooms in the house stayed locked.

Heller wanted Trice to forget about the "sanatorium", to be lulled into a dull complacency and assume everything was running smoothly. She wanted him to concentrate on improvements to his machine and not worry about Larkin.

Nevertheless, after two weeks Larkin was getting itchy.

"Doc, when can ah get out o' hyeh? Ah need a drag and ah need it bad. Ah done had enough o' this joint."

"Another week or two I believe. Be patient. We'll be ready for the bulk of our consumption patients in another three weeks and I intend to release you before they start arriving." Dr. Whiteman had learned to play along. He still thought Larkin was a nut case. He must be somebody with important information to get this kind of treatment. "We'll see that you get to Lawrence right away."

"Mah plan was tah be in Appleton ahead o' time so ah can case the joint. Ah have tah be ready."

"We'll see to it that you are," Whitman replied. What was this fantasy all about?

"Hey doc, who owns that hay burner out front? Ah seen two machines, a Model M Caddy and a Crawford. One of 'em yours?"

"They belong to the sanatorium."

"Can ah go for a ride in the Caddy? Ah need some fresh air in mah face. Feels like ah'm in the pokey hyeh."

"I'll ask Miss Jensen if you can." At least Larkin had an eye for antique cars.

The cars were used to shuttle Trice, Heller, and the others between the front door and the street.

Before long it was September 30, the day before Larkin's interview. Drugged or not, he couldn't stand his captivity much longer. He had to get out somehow and get to Lawrence University.

"Doc Whiteman, yah said yah would have me out of hyeh in time for mah interview tomorrow. How about it?"

"I don't think I'll have an OK from Dr. Ernst."

"Yah planin' to screw me over? That teaching job could be mah future. Pa'don my French but ah'm fixin' ta get the hell out of this joint whether ya like it or not. Ah've had quite plenty."

"Let me talk to Ernst and I'll see what I can do." My word, Whiteman thought, this guy is really wrapped up in his fantasy world. He's getting way too riled up and needs to be more sedated.

Whiteman asked Trice, "I thought Larkin would be out of here by now. He wants to know when you will release him."

"Not for another week or so."

This fellow must have some incredibly valuable information Whiteman thought if the agency is going to so much trouble to cater to his mental illness.

Drugged or not, Larkin couldn't stand his captivity any longer. He had to get out somehow.

From here on Larkin would be more heavily sedated and kept in a twilight sleep until October 12, the day he would be prepared for the reverse exchange that would take place in the afternoon of the 13th.

The morning of Friday October 11 Heller "accidentally" failed to slip the white powder into Larkin's coffee before the nurse took it to him. He would be more alert than usual that day. Would he take the bait? She made a tour of the building to be sure every door was locked except the dorm room, porch, gym, kitchen, dining room, pantry, and second floor bathroom. She also made certain the hidden surveillance cameras at each building entrance and the front gate were working. Then she stepped out on the porch to talk to Ian.

"Hello Mr. Larkin. I'm looking for your two roommates. Did you have enough for breakfast this morning? The pantry is unlocked if you want anything more."

"No thank yah Miss Jensen."

"Oh Mr. Brinker and Mr. Danbury," she called. "Dr. Ernst would like to see you in his examining room." Heller had conveniently scheduled a meeting to go over the plan for Larkin's return.

After they left, Larkin, a bit more clear-headed than before, pretended he was going to the bathroom. The coast was clear. Sure enough, he went into the pantry to look for bread and fruit to take with him. He snuck down the hall, trying as many doors as he could looking for a place to hide, but almost every door was locked. This is a strange place, he thought. The same two cars are usually in front, the rooms are locked, and where are the patients? Where is all the staff? Something sure didn't add up. Was he the subject of some bizarre medical experiment? He needed to get out, but not through the front or back doors…

What an unexpected surprise it was when Heller, Brinker, and Danbury returned and there was no trace of Larkin. At least, Heller pretended it was a big surprise.

She figured he would head for the pantry first. That's where she expected to find him when the time came, but first she had some business to attend to. She instructed Brinker and Danbury, "Wait here in case he comes back. If he does, one of you come to find me. I'll have a look around." Instead, she went to a closet and got out her cell phone.

In was time for Heller to put her plan into action. Her next step was to contact the Vice President and make her move on Trice and Heinrich.

"Mr. Bentler, I have to inform you that Trice let Larkin escape. If he isn't found and sent back right away it could be catastrophic. The future of the time machine is at stake."

"Is Trice looking for him? What is he doing?"

"Trice doesn't even know he's missing. I'll have to find Larkin myself. I told you Trice shouldn't be running this project. Why don't you put me in charge and have Larkin report to me? He should be concentrating on getting the machine fully operational and certified for use. I can be of great use to you, sir. Samicki, the historian and time traveler, is too close to Trice and he has the mind of a child. You need a historian who understands what you want, and I've made a hobby out of American history. I'm the only one you can rely on to travel to the past and do what you need to have done. You should sack Samicki as soon as the machine is certified."

"I'm the one who will make those decisions, thank you, and I don't need your opinion. Right now, you'd better find Larkin and find him fast or you will be the one who gets sacked. Does Heinrich know about any of this?"

"He'll find out next week," she replied sarcastically. "He only knows what his underlings tell him in his weekly briefings. Why don't you trust me to take care of this matter? You don't need Heinrich."

"Heinrich is *my* business. I suggest you find Larkin and make it quick. I have enough other things to worry about."

But Heller couldn't find him anywhere, either, and his drugs would be completely wearing off soon. There was no sign of him in the surveillance camera recordings. She would be forced to tell Trice and call out a dragnet. They had less than a day to get him back. She called on Brinker, Danbury, and everyone in the building to search the grounds.

Chapter Thirteen
Many Happy Returns

The return exchange was now delayed by at least a day. Eryk knew to stay put in his room and wait, but in less than a day and a half he would be forced to board a train. Nobody would know his coordinates, there could be no return exchange, he would be a captive of the early twentieth century, and history would be irrevocably altered.

Unbeknownst to anyone else, Brinker and Danbury took the precaution of planting hidden bugs in various locations in and around the building. After all, it was their job to track Larkin and they had to cover their backsides. If anything went wrong, Heller wouldn't hesitate to throw them under the bus.

"Stanley, I'm going upstairs and ask the computer to scan today's audio tapes for unusual sounds. Do you want to examine the grounds around the walls for footprints and broken branches? We only have the main and service entrances miked, so if he climbed over the wall, he'll be hard to find. Maybe we should call the police to look for an escaped and unpredictable psycho who thinks he was born a hundred and fifty years ago."

"Better wait and see if we can track him inside first. Nobody wants any publicity about what we're doing here and it would get us fired. If a reporter gets one look inside this place it will be a big story we don't like."

"He's been missing for four hours already. I don't think we can wait much longer. You should have bugged the bread in the pantry."

"It *is* bugged. Authentic eighteenth-century roaches."

"Put your phone on vibrate. I'll buzz you if I find anything."

"Same here."

"What size feet does he wear?"

"Didn't look but his shoes have smooth leather soles and no tread."

Two and a half hours later Brink's search found nothing. Danbury heard what he thought might be a window screen opening and closing on the kitchen recording followed by some scraping noises and a faint, dull thud. He checked the microphones in the other rooms for the ten minutes after the kitchen noises. The only other suspicious noises were two metallic rapping noises near the front entrance two minutes later. The front and service entrance bugs didn't pick up anything unusual. Recordings from the past three hours, after the search started, would be swamped with meaningless noise from the searchers, so there was not much point in examining them.

"Stan, he might have gone out the kitchen window, slid down the post and headed for the front entrance."

"Do you know if the cars have been in or out or if the front gate was opened this morning?"

"I'll check on it."

"There were no smooth footprints or bare feet near the walls. I hope he didn't go over the wall. The searchers on the grounds messed it up. They don't know how to look for broken twigs, climbing marks on trees, scratches along the ground, food scraps, or any of the other signs, and then they leave marks of their own. I'll talk to some of them, see if they saw anything in front."

Shortly thereafter they compared notes.

"Nobody noticed anything. The cars haven't moved and the gate hasn't been opened. None of the surveillance cameras along the wall show anything."

By then it was early evening.

"I think he probably took off from the kitchen to the front gate. Let's check around the cars and in the trees in front," Oliver suggested.

Then they found him. He was cleverly hiding in the storage compartment under the back seat of the Crawford, waiting for it to drive off the grounds.

"Now what?" Danbury asked.

"Let Heller stew for a while. I think she set us up and I don't want to take the rap for this little caper. Let's take him back to the pantry and let them all sweat it out for a while."

By this time Trice was in full panic mode, though it didn't show. He was outwardly stoic, calm, and fully self-controlled.

Finally, they took Larkin to Trice and then informed Heller.

A day was lost. There wasn't a second to waste. Trice put his plan in motion at once. He had the agency's mind control expert induce Larkin into a hypnotic state where he remained. Then he was told to go through and rehearse in his mind over and over again all of the events described in his 1907 journal. To that they added all of the pictures, details, and personalities of Appleton and Lawrence, and all of the local events that transpired in September and early October they knew about from their research.

Everyone hoped that by the end of a grueling night and morning, an exhausted Larkin would feel and believe he had lived in Appleton for a month, and that he went to an interview at Lawrence but was not offered the instructor position he hoped for. He was told that the sanatorium was nothing more than an ephemeral dream that he would quickly forget, erased forever from his mind.

When they woke him up from the trance, he was told he would be waking up from a nap in his room at the boarding house. There he was instructed to look around and find a ticket he had bought to St. Louis for the morning of the 15th. He was commanded to arrive at the station early, in plenty of time to board his train.

Would the hypnotic trance take? They were hopeful. It had worked before on all but a handful of the agency's most obstinate captives.

The instant the trance was lifted, Larkin was whisked into the time machine where the countdown to the reverse transfer resumed.

Then suddenly, the instant Larkin disappeared, Eryk materialized. A weary Trice immediately started the debriefing of a startled Eryk Samicki. Time was of the essence in case there had been a breach of history.

* * *

Heller rang up an angry Bentler to tell him the search was successful, thanks to her. "Mr. Bentler, I was on top of this from the beginning and organized the search right away. We found Larkin. He was processed and sent back. I think we should move on reshuffling project management as soon as Trice finishes his final test."

"You deceived me, Heller," Bentler practically screamed at her. "Now I know I can't trust you."

"Mr. Bentler, I assure you I would never mislead you. There is some mistake here."

"Yes, there *is* a mistake and you made it. Did you think Brinker and Danbury worked for *you*? They're the best in the business. I know all about how Larkin's escape came about. It was your scheme to take over the project. Tell me one reason why I shouldn't have you arrested and sent to one of your own agency's interrogation camps to disappear once and for all."

"You know we're two of a kind. Please give me another chance," she begged.

"No, we are *not* two of a kind," Bentler said emphatically. "I have all the evidence I need to have you apprehended for aiding and abetting a fugitive, or terminated for insubordination, or whatever I happen to feel like doing with you. You are a marked woman, living with a black cloud over your head. And why didn't you implant an

RFID chip into Larkin the moment he arrived so you wouldn't lose him?"

"We couldn't risk returning him with it."

"You're on probation with me. You have a lot of groveling and hard work to do if you ever want to redeem yourself. Just how do you think you can prove to me I can rely on you? And if you can't, you can contemplate the fact that your career will be prematurely shortened. From now on, you exist entirely at my pleasure and you will do exactly as I tell you to, understood?" "Yes, sir, understood," she chafed.

* * *

Eryk's mind was totally preoccupied with looking up his almost-girlfriend's history and finding a way to go back to Appleton to see her.

"Eryk! Eryk! Are you with me?" Oh dear, an exhausted Trice thought. Time travel scrambled his brain.

"Huh? Oh, professor."

"You're back. We have to debrief right now. If anything changed, if anything went wrong, we have to fix it immediately."

"Yes, Appleton. Have you noticed anything different?"

"I can't, that's the problem. If history changed, the people who came later and their recollections would change to match. Nobody alive can have any knowledge of how things were before the time travel, because they would all be part of the new reality. You, the time traveler, are the only person who can tell if anything was altered, and you can only tell based on your memory and knowledge of history before you left. Wrack your brain. I have to depend on you."

"Ferber, I have to see if she still wrote the books I remember.

And the baseball scores, are they still the same? I'd better check historical events, presidents, wars, everything I know about the history of the last hundred years."

"Where's the journal?"

"I decided to leave it at the boarding house. I couldn't find Larkin's original journal anywhere and we agreed that if he had it with him you would keep it."

"He didn't have it."

"Then where is it? It wasn't in Appleton that I could find. Let's check our original in the archives, the historical artifact." An hour later, they compared notes.

"One of the World Series scores is different," Eryk said. "It might mean trouble. Ferber's books and all the major historical milestones check out so far."

"The journal in our archives is the fake one!" Trice exclaimed. "Now I know for sure history was changed. There have to be more repercussions, but what, where? You have to dredge up everything you can remember and check on it, right now! This is nerve-wracking. There's nothing I can do and it's all up to you. We need a plan to fix this."

"Get Sandy to help me. If what you say is true and nobody alive can have any recollection of an alternative history, it means none of your carefully thought-out contingency plans are any good."

"I know that now. And if the time traveler never returned, or if he came back to a world that was destroyed, the new history would irrevocably be the new reality. It's the discontinuity you talked about. The time traveler is the key and the only hope if things go awry."

"What does that mean?"

"Next time the machine has to be programmed for an automatic return. There has to be a way to force the exchanged person to be in the machine in time. Travel to the past has to be a quick and surgical operation, with a procedure to be strictly followed and adhered to. One day, one action, then return. Small steps, one at a time, one single objective per mission. That will be the new plan."

"Next time."

"You know, Eryk, if you went back in time and saved millions of people nobody would ever know it except you yourself. Nobody would ever know anything about the terrible alternate history you prevented. You would be an unsung hero because if you ever told anybody what you did, they would just lock you up."

As Eryk was verifying the historical record, he couldn't help but be reminded of Trice's tirades about ruthless dictators. Many hundreds of them throughout human history, narcissistic powerseeking sociopaths who were frequently a mix of bloodthirsty, extremist, and power-seeking warmongers, architects of wars, systematic and mass murders, bloody genocides, torture, and much more.

Hitler was responsible for an estimated 17 million deaths. Stalin caused the deaths of between 2.6 million and 10 million people through execution, starvation, and torture, including the period of his "Great Purge." Mao Zedong systematically killed between 4 and 6 million people through executions and forced labor camps. His mass repressions included minimum execution quotas. The infamous Pol Pot murdered, or rather "cleansed," a fifth of the Cambodian population, between 1.7 to 2.5 million of them, some through starvation.

In Africa Mengistu Haile Mariam of Ethiopia smothered President Haile Selassie and instigated the Ethiopian Red Terror, responsible for the mass murder and torture of 1.5 million. Yakubu Gowon of Nigeria starved more than a million civilians and killed a hundred thousand soldiers.

Elsewhere, Ismail Enver Pasha needed a scapegoat for his military losses and blamed the Armenians, accompanied by a policy of mass genocide against them. Leopold II of Belgium pursued a colonial empire, pressing African populations into forced labor during which they were badly abused. Vlad III the Impaler was unfortunately easily offended and didn't hesitate to maim, torture, and kill anyone and everyone who displeased him.

The list was endless. Add to that tens of thousands of unprincipled psychopaths inspiring others to join them in their murdering, bombing, and looting, and ruining the lives of countless additional victims.

What if Trice was right and these so-called people could be stopped? Did they have a moral obligation to try? Or would the attempt just be a fruitless, never-ending game of whack-a-mole as countless other psychos and sociopaths sprang up to fill the void? Would repeated trips to the past to try to eradicate them all turn the fabric of history into so much dryer lint?

Maybe in the end, humanity would finally be forced to return to the past and find out in one final desperate experiment to save itself.

Chapter Fourteen
Capture

Ever since the reception, Trice was mesmerized by Eryk's wife. He knew better but it didn't matter. It all started with her flirting. Trice took it seriously. Such beautiful women had never noticed him before. Trice couldn't wait to call Natalie Samicki and try to meet her in private. He made certain Eryk was insanely busy with preparations and training for his upcoming time travel.

On the Tuesday following the reception, Trice called Natalie from work. "Hi Natalie. Is it alright for me to call you that? Eryk is busy with a training session tonight and he won't be home until late. Can I drop by your place? I'm off now."

"Darling, I'm famished. Why don't we meet at a cozy little restaurant somewhere and get better acquainted."

Yes, of course, he was being too forward. He should be more patient. "You have no idea how excited I am to see you again. I can be there in half an hour."

"What about your wife? Eryk says you're married."

"She assumes I'm working late again. She knows how much pressure I'm under to finish my project."

"Your top secret project?"

"Yes, unfortunately. I can't tell her about it. You either."

"How convenient. There's a cute little Italian place near 17th and Prospect. Look for me there."

"See you soon."

The next morning Natalie was working but Trice kept trying to call her until she finally arrived home.

"Hi Natalie. I couldn't wait to talk to you and see you again. I've never enjoyed being with anyone before the way I do with you."

"I told you not to call me. I'll let you know when I can talk."

"But Eryk is busy with a research report. It's due by tonight. He won't be home until ten or eleven."

"You know my signal. When I have time for *you*, you'll be the first to know."

"Alright, alright. What does your schedule look like?"

"Didn't I just tell you I would let you know? Maybe I can fit you in tomorrow around six. Is that OK with you?"

"Certainly. Same place as last time?"

"Where else?"

"Why don't we go over to your place afterwards? I can make sure Eryk won't get home until midnight."

"No, I don't want to do that."

And that was the start of it. Several weeks later on a Tuesday Trice's cell phone buzzed twice, stopped, and buzzed twice again. That was Natalie's signal to call her on her at home.

He found a vacant office and called her right back. "Did you call me?"

"No, you just called me. I didn't have time for lunch today. I need something especially good to eat tonight. I want you to meet me at the Adelphi Restaurant at six thirty sharp, will you do that for me?"

"That's a very expensive place."

"Why are you complaining? Don't you want to show me how special I am?"

"Of course you are. We've been meeting for more than three weeks now. Don't you think our relationship should be progressing?"

"Darling, neither one of us should be risking that under the circumstances. I have to go now. Don't be late."

After emptying his wallet on a first-class meal, Trice said, "Natalie, Dear. Can I call you Dear? Don't you think it's time to find a hotel somewhere out of the way? I think we're ready for the next step. You know what I mean."

"Randolph, darling, you're not dumb enough to think this is a serious relationship, are you? It's all a pastime. I've been bored. Aren't you? Aren't you tired of working so much? Don't you get it? You're my play toy. This is a game between the two of us, that's all."

"But I thought there was something special between us. I don't understand. You've made yourself available. I thought I was important to you."

"You shouldn't assume things like that. You're as much of a loser as my so-called husband. I'll bet I'm your only social contact outside of work. I'm just having fun, nothing else. How could you possibly imagine there's anything more to it than that? You need to get a life."

"I put my security clearance and my marriage at risk for you. You have to know that. Doesn't it mean anything to you?"

"You're boring me. Why don't you pay the check, or buy yourself a drink and pay the check. I'm leaving. Don't call me again. I'll call you if I want to see you, but frankly, I'm getting pretty damn bored with you." Just like that, she walked out.

"Waitress," he said as he flagged her down. "Which house wines do you recommend?"

Ten minutes later he hadn't touched his glass. "Sir, don't you like our wine?" she asked Trice.

"Just bring me the check," he replied. He thought to himself, maybe it was better not to go home with alcohol on his breath. He paid the bill and slinked home, thoroughly demoralized and depressed. He knew he would be having no more enticing romantic fantasies for a while.

Meanwhile, Heller's eagle eyes didn't miss Natalie's flirting at the reception and Trice's falling for it. Certainly, she would find a way to take advantage of it. She grabbed Watkins at work the next chance she had. "Sandy, I have an important job for you. Don't tell anyone about it and don't ask me any questions. Can you agree to that?"

"Yes, you know you can depend on me."

"I'm worried that Trice will do something to compromise the security of the project. That would be terrible since he's the brains behind the machine. There's a security guard here who moonlights as a detective. He agreed to keep an eye on Trice but we need your help. There will be times when he needs you to follow Trice from a distance and take pictures of whoever he meets with. Are you willing to help?"

"Yes, of course."

"Good. He'll provide you with a pair of digital binoculars and a compact long range amplified digital camera. You have to be discreet and stay hidden. Make sure you get good pictures. He'll call you whenever he needs your assistance."

"OK."

*　*　*

Upon Eryk's return, Heller had the opportunity to put her information to good use. It didn't matter that nothing physical happened between Trice and Natalie. Her imagination was ready to expand a few weeks into an epic liaison and fill in a few appropriate erotic details for effect. She was lying in wait for Eryk when his four days of intensive debriefing finally concluded.

"Eryk, there's something you should know. While you were busy studying and training and preparing for your time travel and the entire time you were gone, your boss and so-called friend Trice was screwing your wife. Didn't you wonder why you were always working late when he wasn't?"

"I don't believe you."

"I have witnesses. You want some evidence?"

"And just why were you paying such close attention to what he was doing? Did you stage it? I know how you roll. If there was anything going on you must have set it up."

"You want a list of the times and places where they met? I'll be happy to give you one and you can ask Trice about it yourself."

"Who else have you been spying on?"

"I told you I should be the one selecting the time traveler and now you understand why. You said yourself time travel can be murderous. It should be my job to make sure only moral, ethical, history conscious individuals make the trip."

"In other words, nobody like you."

"Why don't you see for yourself?"

The seed was planted. Eryk knew he would be compelled to follow up on it, and he had no choice but to confront his boss. After working hours was the right time, when the two of them would continue their analysis of the trip, off the record.

"Heller says you're having an affair with my wife."

"I'm sorry Eryk. We met a couple of times for dinner after work. Nothing more than that."

"Without telling me? How could you fall for her flirting? How could you betray me like that?"

"It was a mistake and I'm sorry. I hope it won't affect our working relationship."

"How can you think it won't? How can you think I will ever trust you again? Now I can't stand either one of you."

"I don't blame you. Please just give me a chance to make it up to you. I value our relationship."

"That's not what it looks like to me."

"I know. Believe me, she taught me a lesson."

"I'm sure she did. I hate to lose our friendship and our close working relationship, but how can I possibly avoid it?"

It felt like real, maybe permanent, damage had been done. He reminded himself Natalie was surely the instigator, same as always. It just confirmed what he already knew: his marriage was a disaster and he needed to get out of it, to file for divorce if he had to, yet he wasn't ready to let go, at least not quite yet.

Heller pressed her hand the next day. "Alright, Eryk, as far as I'm concerned you really work for me now and that's how you should look at it yourself. You're through with Trice and I have a different agenda in mind for this project."

"You're crazy."

"Look, either you play ball or I tell everybody here about Trice's affair. The both of you will be ashamed to show you faces around here ever again."

"Forget it."

"I'll tell Trice's wife about it and present her with the evidence if I have to. I'll wreck their marriage and I'll ruin the both of you. They'll revoke his security clearance, maybe yours, too."

"I can't believe you would stoop that low."

"Why wouldn't I be? I'll get what I want in the end, so you may as well go along for your own sake."

"Owned by *two* devils? No way."

"Don't pretend you're so pure. That's for children. Why don't you leave your ivory tower for a change? Take a vacation in the real world."

That made everything crystal clear. Eryk determined to work with Trice to stop Heller even if the personal touch was gone. Maybe protecting the project would help restore their relationship, at least he hoped so. Most people realized Heller was an office snake, as Trice was about to find out for himself.

And it didn't take long. Heller was working both sides of the room.

"Trice, I know all about you and Eryk's wife. I want Eryk out of the program. You will get rid of him immediately. I will be the new time traveler along with my current position, since I'm the best qualified."

"Eryk already has practical experience at it. You don't."

"Listen, like it or not, from now on, I'm calling the shots, do you understand? If you don't do what I say, I'll tell your wife about you and your girlfriend in full sexual detail if you know what I mean. I have the evidence to back it up. You could easily get yourself fired over this."

"Are you that depraved?"

"It's life, not depravity. Get used to it. You know what I expect you to do. I will get Bentler's full backing on this."

"You know perfectly well that without me there *is* no project. You'll have nothing to be in charge of."

"We'll see, won't we?"

"You're disgusting," Trice responded. "It's my machine and I won't be blackmailed."

He was, of course, quite worried nonetheless. It was now clear that Heller had no boundaries,

Eryk was sure now he wanted to escape back to Appleton to be with the woman he really cared about. How nice it would be if he never had to deal with Natalie's shenanigans or with Heller again. Surely, he could work out a way to manage the consequences and not damage anyone, but how could he influence Trice's plan for the final test? And just to make certain he wasn't a bigamist or a cheater, he intended to change history one way or another so that he and Natalie never met. Should he just be open with Trice about it? If he did that, Trice would probably transfer him off the project, then cave in to Heller's blackmail and her demands to be the time traveler. Eryk didn't want to stoop to trickery. While he thought it over, he continued researching his wife's family tree; it was all just a matter of some time travel and a train trip.

Did it come down to a choice between a time traveler with evil intent (Heller) versus another traveler with a personal rather than a humanitarian motive (himself)? Did morality come down to choosing the least unethical path? Would his plan and his intentions have to remain a secret that he dares not mention, lest someone else unleash a self-serving catastrophe on future humanity? Eryk struggled to find a way.

* * *

Instead playing defense with a poor hand, it was time for Trice and Eryk to cook up some ideas of their own. Like preparing a plate of unanticipated consequences for Heller.

"Before we come up with a strategy, I suggest you change all of the access codes," Eryk suggested. "Nobody should know them but you. That way they have to keep you around."

"No, I haven't. That would violate policy."

"My recommendation is to do it anyway, and disable your biometrics while you're at it. Even iris scans can be faked. This agency does it all the time."

"That's a dangerous action for me to take."

"So what will they do? Fire you? Demote you to a GS-1 scrub lady position? They can't if they want their machine. You need the security. In my opinion, we don't want anyone else to be in a position of taking over. It's not just Heller I'm worried about. Dauer wants to control the machine and take charge of the project, the Vice President is scrutinizing ever minute aspect of the machine, and we don't know who else secretly knows about it and wants to use it for some personal gain."

"Let's think, who else might know about it outside this department, the agency director, and the vice president?" Trice questioned.

"They're the only ones I can think of for sure. No telling if Heinrich has loose lips about the project. It looks to me like Watkins has been snooping around for a while now. Let's find him and put some pressure on him. I want to find out what he knows and who he's spying for, as if we can't guess."

"I don't think Heller is working on her own. She's the type who will look for secret allies to help her, then set them up and double-cross them when it's to her advantage."

"Why can't you play the same trick on her? Why not pretend to cave in to her blackmail and agree for her to be the time traveler, but secretly change the codes to send her to some desert island a hundred year from now. You can be humane and make sure there are pineapple trees there."

"Maybe, but she's the type who dots all the i's and crosses all the t's. She would probably figure it out. I think she would insist I transfer you somewhere else first."

"There must be a way you can fake it."

Trice went to get Watkins.

"Sandy," he asked, "we think you've been watching us and reporting everything to someone like Heller. How about it?"

"I'm just following orders. What else can I do?"

"Is it Heller? You know she doesn't need you anymore. She'll sack you the next chance she gets."

"I know you're right, but I was hoping she would be grateful," he replied dejectedly.

"Why? What did she promise you?"

"Nothing. She told me I had to do it. I didn't have a choice. She's watching everybody. What will you do with me?"

"Nothing. We expect you to do your job to the best of your ability and keep us informed about anything we need to know and everything Heller tells you to do, in private of course. Don't tell Heller or anybody else we're onto you."

"Yeah, sure," Watkins replied slowly, looking straight at the floor.

Eryk and Trice no longer had any confidence in Watkins. They would have to be careful around him and not give him any critical assignments.

"I'm afraid we'll have to keep an eye on *you* now."

"Yeah, I know, I need a drink," Watkins muttered as he slinked out the door. It looked to him like everybody wanted to fire him and any minute now.

Eryk asked Trice, "Maybe Watkins could be useful. What misinformation can we feed him?"

* * *

"Dauer, have you written down how the machine works like I told you to?" Heller asked.

"Dauer is working on it. The physics is difficult."

"Do you want to take over for Trice or not? I want your work finished right away. You have to understand it well enough to explain all of the details to another scientist you might need to assist you. You're no use to me or to the project if you can't do at least that."

"Dauer can do it."

"Don't let me down. This is urgent. It's your highest priority and I won't wait on you much longer."

"Well, there is a problem. Somebody changed the access codes to the time machine. Dauer can't set up the operating parameters or examine the software."

"I thought you said you knew everything about the machine."

"Yes, don't worry, Dauer can find out the codes again." Did he really have a clue how to hack the machine?

Heller had to update the Vice President.

"Sir, let's be perfectly frank with each other. You need me to run the time machine project. I don't see anyone else you can rely on.

I know you intend to move up to the presidency and consolidate your power, and I want to ride your coat tails. Let's make a deal."

"The deal is, if you do what I tell you to, you won't get sacked and arrested. Clear?"

"I'll consider that a deal."

"The deal lasts only for as long as you give me what I want."

"There's a problem but I'm working on it. Trice changed all the security codes to the machine. Nobody else has access now."

"Just what are you doing about it?"

"Dauer says he knows how to break into the machine."

"He'd better or he'll be the mystery meat at the next big barbeque."

How can I get something on Bentler, Heller asked herself? She must think. Her future ascendancy depended on it. He was ostensibly married but there were plenty of rumors about him. His bodyguards protected him, an obstacle she had to work around. Maybe there was a way to hook him up with Natalie Samicki and keep the two of them together. A light bulb went off.

"I have a backup plan," she told Bentler. "We might be able to get to the codes through Eryk Samicki. Maybe you can have a discreet meeting with his wife and use some of that charm you have. You met her before, do you remember?"

"I remember the tart."

"Once we have the codes and Dauer knows enough about the machine, we can get rid of Trice and anyone loyal to him."

"Why don't you let me decide that? You're back on thin ice again. I'm becoming really impatient with you. Get the security codes. I don't want to hear any more of your problems, only the solutions. I can't wait much longer for the machine."

"You won't have to wait for long Mr. Bentler, I can assure you of that. You can help by hooking up with Natalie Samicki. Please consider it."

"Do you know what happened to Theodore Roosevelt? He was a thorn in the side of the New York bosses so they kicked him upstairs to vice president to get rid of him. Then you know what happened? Somebody shot President McKinley a month after he took office and Roosevelt was in charge of the whole damned country. He had an image. People loved him. They would do anything he wanted.

"That's what's about to happen again. When I'm in charge the political handlers and bosses will be gone. No more. I won't even have a wipe-ass vice president to deal with. Don't let me down."

Chapter Fifteen
An Unsolved Puzzle

"You deserted me for over a month and you expect me to welcome you back? You never called, not once. I didn't even get a postcard from you."

"It was a worthwhile trip. I learned a lot and it was very helpful to Trice. I went to a remote place and it was impossible to contact you."

"How do I know that? You went to a remote place in a hotel room with some bimbo. Trice fixed you up. He's your pimp."

"It was strictly business, Agency business."

"Yeah, sure. It was monkey business. I know, I have a sixth sense. Why do you always think you can fool me? It's so insulting."

"Suppose I went on a spy mission in a foreign country. How could I contact you without risking my life?"

"You couldn't make just one little phone call? Of course you could. Besides, you'll never be a spy and it wasn't some secret spy mission. You were with some tramp in an out-of-the-way place somewhere the whole time, I can tell. Trice set it up to get you out of his face for a while."

"It was official business."

"Then prove it. How dumb do you think I am? You're being stupid if you think you can get away with it."

"I can't offer you proof. What we do is top secret. You want me to go to jail for divulging state secrets?"

"If you cared about me, you'd prove it, I don't care how secret you claim it was. Maybe you got her pregnant. Then it wouldn't be so secret anymore."

"Ask Trice or Sandy if you want. I can arrange to have them talk to you."

"I don't need to talk to anyone. I know."

Just like old times. Now Eryk really felt like he was back and it was real.

As soon as he could manage it Eryk was online again looking up his wife's cousins, parents, brothers and sister, everyone from 1900 onward, and he was committing the details to memory. That included what each of them did, the places they lived, their spouses and the spouses' family trees, and if he could find out, which ones associated with whom, and which ones had no contact with each other. He was determined to find out where he could go back to and switch the tracks so Natalie would never have met him in the first place.

What were the critical points, places, and times he could alter? He was about to return to the past one more time and he didn't want to blow the opportunity.

Eryk also looked up Vera Bleeker. She continued to live with her mother until her graduation from Lawrence in 1910 at the age of twenty-six. After graduation she taught English for four and a half years in Columbus, Wisconsin and Oak Park, Illinois. Her salary enabled her to embark on her dream of traveling through Europe during her breaks from school. She went to France, England, and Scotland. Sadly, she died of typhoid fever in 1915, one of around twenty who were infected at the school where she taught. She was only thirty. Her beloved brother named his first child, a daughter born in 1915, after her.

Eryk thought, what if he had spent her precious few years with her? Maybe if they had traveled together, she wouldn't have gotten sick and died so young. He missed her so much now.

* * *

Bentler wasn't the kind to rely on others. He had to be in full control of everything himself, at all times. Now he would do whatever he had to and seize the machine. His patience was spent.

He was determined to get the codes himself before anyone else did. Then he would have sole control of the time machine. No doubt, there were plenty of physicists and computer experts around he could tap. One is as good as another. He didn't have to rely on Heller. Heller, Heinrich, Dauer, Trice, and Samicki were all expendable liabilities.

He had his trusted personal secretary arrange a date with Natalie Samicki in a safe, cozy, and discreet restaurant that would thoroughly impress her. A limo would pick her up from a parking lot where nobody would notice.

Natalie couldn't wait. The Vice President, the second most powerful man in the world in her estimation, had noticed her. She thought to herself, "This is the big time, my greatest challenge ever. Catch this one and I'll be set for life." It never occurred to her how far out of her league she was. Finally, it was her turn to get played.

* * *

Watkins was a ghost, a shell of a man. The people he worked for, the ones whose opinions he courted and counted on, all hated him for sure. All of them avoided him and nobody trusted him with anything important to do. He wished he could be somebody else, anybody. His only consolation was at the bottom of a bottle.

Could he make a last-ditch effort to ingratiate himself with Trice, he wondered?

"Heller and Bentler talk all the time," he offered Trice. "I'm trying to hang around and catch as much of it as I can. They're planning something and it involves the time machine. I think you should be looking over your shoulder."

"Do you really want to get back in my good graces?"

"Yes! How?"

"Your work has been getting sloppy. I want you to shape up."

"I'll try. What do you want me to do?"

Trice was ready to slow Heller down by planting a little misinformation, something to embarrass her with the Vice President. He was sure he couldn't trust Watkins and he had to be careful.

"I'm going to give you a special research assignment. I want you to call and to report your progress to me every other day. You don't have to avoid Heller when you call me, but don't tell her what you're working on. If she asks just say it's background for the final test mission."

"OK. What's the mission?"

"I'm setting the machine to go back right after the president's election to his first term, during his first two weeks in office. I want you to research everything the new president did and said, everywhere he went, who he was with, what he did, everything during those first two weeks. Can you accept the assignment?"

"Yes. I won't let you down this time."

"Thank you. I'll be waiting for your progress reports."

Of course, that was not where the final time travel test would go at all, but here was a chance to put some egg on Heller's face and find out what the two of them were up to. Heller was always carefully watching everyone. She was sure to take the bait.

* * *

"Sandy, I see you working on something," Heller said. "Did Trice give you an assignment? You promised to keep me informed."

"Please, Trice told me not to tell you what I'm doing."

"And who are you going to listen to?"

"You, of course," he replied sheepishly.

As soon as Watkins spilled the beans, Heller wanted to give Bentler an update.

"Sir, Trice is planning his next mission to coincide with the president's first two weeks in office. I'm sure he's up to something."

"What are you trying to tell me?" Bentler raged. "Brinker and Danbury listened in on Eryk saying he was going back to the early 1900s again. I can't trust you for a single minute, can I?"

"I swear, Watkins heard it from Trice himself. He's spent the last three weeks researching the period. I forced him to tell me about it. He wouldn't be wasting his time with that kind of research if the trip was going anywhere else. Maybe Eryk doesn't know himself. Maybe he's just assuming."

"I thought Trice and Samicki were tight?"

"Not since Samicki found out Trice was seeing his wife."

"You'd better be right about this. You know, Heller, history will record that the president was another McKinley. When I take over nobody will oppose me and you know why? They won't survive. That's what the time machine is for. I wouldn't have put up with you or Trice or funded the project otherwise. If I have the machine, I can be the most powerful man who ever lived. Anyone who gets in my way will die or never be born in the first place. There will be a coup d'état around here the instant the machine is proven. If I can't trust you by then, maybe you'll be the final test and you can cool your heels in sixth century Siberia."

"I'm here to help you with your plan. I will always be dedicated to your success."

"Please. You're dedicated to *me*? That's how you intend to show me I can trust you? How does that help me? I have a mind to put you in charge of setting up and running a labor camp in an isolated spot near the Arctic Circle. It would suit your talents perfectly, don't you think? That way I won't have to watch you all the time. Whatever you do with the prisoners will be your business. No doubt you'll come up with a way to use them for your own personal profit."

"I think you need me to gain control of the machine, and who else has the historical knowledge to be your time traveler?"

"If I send *you*, I'll have to send somebody else to watch you because there's no telling what that twisted little snake-brain of yours will come up with. I'm sure you have your own personal agenda to take over, and it might even involve getting rid of *me*. You're not the one. I need to send an assassin I can trust, someone who's not smart enough to concoct his own plan."

"I swear to you I don't have a separate agenda. My best option is riding your coat tails and that's my plan."

"You're trying my patience again. With the machine I can blamelessly wipe out every single one of my political opponents and whoever else I don't like, and no one will be the wiser. I'll have no resistance because anyone who opposes me will be eliminated or sent to a slave labor camp, and nobody will know the difference. I'll have the power to help myself to anything I want and I can decide who deserves to eat and live, and who doesn't. This is so close I can taste it, but then, so can you. Maybe you have the same program for yourself."

Bentler needed to plant a mole and find out the truth about the test mission and Heller's loyalty. Who could he trust? If the trip was indeed going back to the president's first two weeks in office it was an opportunity he couldn't pass up. He called Heinrich.

Here was a mass bloodbath in the making. Several of them.

* * *

"I've made some changes and adjustments to the machine since your time travel," Trice said. "We're ready to go again. Are you all set for your final test trip?"

"Am I returning to September 1907 to fix the history that changed, or continuing on in October? Baseball history changed, and that can't be all. We still have both my personal experience and the research we did before, and I can fix what went wrong last time."

"Neither one. I don't want to risk any more historical accidents no matter how minor they are. You're going back as yourself two years ago. You will simply relive a day from your own past, nothing more. That way, nothing can possibly go wrong. A very simple trip for just over half a day, sixteen hours only. Nothing will fail if the machine works right. What's the matter?"

Eryk's disappointment must have shown. "Nothing. It's just not what I expected." His plan would have to change now. There would barely be enough time to drive his car to Lynchburg and back and do what he needed to do. Nobody would ever be the wiser for it, either. Memories would change. Nobody would ever figure out what he did. It was a perfect crime.

Trice continued. "You're going at seven o'clock tomorrow morning. I've programmed the machine to automatically send you and bring you back. Precisely sixteen hours after you arrive stand in the same spot and wait for your return."

The next morning Trice was in the control room making his final checks and watching the monitors. Where was Heller he wondered? Why wasn't she there? A broad grin crossed Trice's face.

Eryk readied himself for his short mission. The giant capacitors were filling rapidly with their energy, ready for the dramatic near-instantaneous focused discharge. The machine started its countdown to maximum energy concentration: "Ten, nine…"

Just then as the steel door started to close, Eryk saw a heavily armed Brinker and Danbury barge into the observation room, grab Trice, and start to drag him away. "Oh my god!" he thought as a flash of fear engulfed him. Then Eryk disappeared from the machine. The future wouldn't unfold the way he had expected.

Chapter Sixteen
Adventure Postponed

Eryk returned to a very familiar time and place. It was eerie. Here he was again just like before, but this time he knew exactly what his future held in store. It was more than déjà vu.

What would happen if the time machine failed now? Most likely he would either die or be stuck in limbo, in some kind of a twilight.

Eryk knew what he had to do. He knew what the security codes had been at the time of his trip and he logged onto Trice's account. Eryk changed the specifications and CAD drawings for the time machine's cooling pumps so their capacity would be completely inadequate. Then he tried to mentally prepare himself for his own death, expected in another few hours when the machine failed. He relived in his mind the time he spent with Vera and Lyell. He remembered how she looked, how she talked, what they did together, and he smiled, her image fresh before his eyes. It would fully occupy his mind and be the last thing he ever remembered.

* * *

It was September again. Director Heinrich and Vice President Bentler were all over Trice to hurry up and finish his time machine.

A tired and disappointed Trice told Eryk "The machine is overheating. Nobody can pinpoint the problem. I know how hard you've worked the past six months studying and preparing for a trip back to 1907, but it just isn't safe to send you. The attempt could even kill you. I'm sorry, I have to cancel the experiment."

Eryk just looked off in the distance and said nothing. "Salut d'amour" echoed throughout his brain. Nobody on earth knew the real story except him. He remembered the love of his life, the woman he wanted to be with, and a baseball score that should have been 2 to 2.

Addendum One
Characters

<u>Dr. Randolph Trice</u> craves order and predictability. If there is anything out of place, unexplainable, or not as it should be, he is overcome by anxiety and he obsesses on gaining control and putting things right again. It's almost as if he would transform the cosmos back to its original state of uniform, predictable, symmetrical perfection if he was able to; after half a lifetime of dedicated hard work he now has a tool to do exactly that, or at least some approximation thereof. What it was in his upbringing that brought about this compulsion for predictable order is open to speculation.

Trice cannot, that is, he doesn't dare, tolerate the threat of dissenters to this sacred and obsessive quest for harmonious predictability. Nor will he consider the possibility of unintended consequences because his vision of a perfectly ordered society is too important to allow him to believe there are any insurmountable obstacles. This unexamined craving shows up in many ways he is not consciously aware of. Trice is not grandiose nor is he angry or volatile. Rather, he tends to be even-keeled, orderly, and predictable just like his ideal society. Because of his desire for predictability, he is very self-controlled and doesn't question this trait which is so obvious to everyone else.

Similarly, if he fails to get a definite answer to a question he poses to a coworker, or if he is around anyone who likes to wing it or play it by ear, or if confronted by poorly thought-out planning, he can get extremely annoyed and impatient, but in a polite sort of way.

But there are, as there must be, contradictory, compensatory forces in the shadows of his mind which are all the more powerful since he is not aware of them. That is, he may once in a great while do or utter something rebellious or unethical without being aware of it.

That action or thought will be rationalized, compartmentalized, or suppressed. In this case, his affair is out of character, but it arises from conscious impulses he dares not to question, lest it makes an internal conflict painfully conscious.

Trice's technical genius, reliability, dedication, and even disposition, gain him a lot of respect and helps to cement his leadership position.

Dr. Eryk Samicki is an armchair explorer of American history. As his married life started to deteriorate from its beginning, he got the feeling it would be curative to get his nose out of the archives and into the field, and to search for some real adventure. Maybe that would somehow reconnect him with the fountain of feeling that was once a common experience for him. His world and his ego were shattering, and he desperately needed a change. The time machine was the ideal conduit, maybe to another place where he might fit in and thrive. He found the possibilities to be mesmerizing. His choice was the same as everyone's, to explore either the inner or the outer world and his projections on to the latter. Every day cares, rules, roles and necessities dictated not only the later path, but it also gave Eryk his appetite to study historic lives, cultures, and times, looking for settings he would feel alive in. At some point in the seemingly distant future, he will in fact discover he has to face his inner conflicts, too, as difficult and painful as that can be, but that time has not yet arrived, and maybe he can continue to avoid it altogether.

Eryk's preoccupation with his immediate predicament sometimes blinds him to the difficulties of others and makes him unintentionally insensitive, and it also robs him of vital energy, a failing he is dimly aware of. Nevertheless, he still retains his curiosity. He is also fairly easy-going, knowledgeable and observant on subjects that interest him, as well as methodical and logical. That means he has a tendency to live in an idealized world, an ivory tower of sorts. He can thus often be abstract and theoretical, and occasionally plainly boring when his thoughts lie somewhere else and he isn't paying full attention to the external world.

Juanita Heller is extremely ambitious and will do whatever she must to advance her position and her career. After all, she is entitled, superior, and owed. She makes no attempt to disguise her intentions because she doesn't see them as aberrant, but instead as being just the reality of things. She is a cool, calculating master manipulator who is adept at playing off her competitors against each other. Nor is she at all hesitant to use and discard anyone who can serve as a tool to further her aims. She immediately starts sizing up anyone she meets to find out if they might be an obstacle, a potential ally (unwitting or strategic), or of no use to her. In the former two cases the sizing-up will be an ongoing preoccupation. A major objective is to identify her competitors' weaknesses and exploit them for the maximum possible personal and political gain. Backing people into a corner so they are forced to either do her bidding or face personal ruin is a stock-in-trade. No demand is too much regardless of the loss others would suffer carrying out her dictates. Getting what she wants is everything. She is never troubled by the ethical issues or guilt that keeps others awake at night. Her ambitious competitors see her as a dangerous barracuda to be quarantined, though that isn't her point of view at all; it's the others who are dangerous. A few office politicians might be tempted to try and hitch a ride, cynically using her drive and ambition to boost themselves up, but if they don't suck up enough and she gets suspicious, she will put a knife in their back.

Natalie Samicki is accustomed to using her superior looks, charm, and flirtatious manner to get whatever she wants. After all, wealth, status, admiration, and homage are her natural due. Her values are whatever she happens to crave at a particular instant in time. She is more or less an automaton. She acts out of impulse and is virtually never aware of what and when her next mood will be, or why it is she demands whatever she thinks it is she wants at any particular moment.

Whatever that is, she is certain she is entitled to immediate satisfaction and everyone else is obligated to help her get it, or to at least stay out of the way. If she imagines that anyone is in her way, her charm will suddenly evaporate and everyone including the recalcitrant will be subject to an erupting volcano of rage.

She learned at an early age that her seductive beauty and calculated cuteness was a potent tool for manipulation, but if that fails, it opens a crack for the normally concealed volcano to erupt. In that case, her impatience and anger are projected and appears to her as other people's self-centered and insensitive intransigence. In other words, she always blames someone else if she doesn't get her way and heaven help them. Once she does get what she wants, as is normally the case, the charming and pleasantly cute front she displays suddenly disappears. As soon as she has hooked her fish, she immediately becomes bored and wants to shed her victim for good.

Underneath she is quite unaware of her own sensitivity and vulnerability to the expressed opinions of others and its accompanying paranoia. The smallest perceived slight sets off a rage and a determination to get even for the outrageous insult she was unjustifiably inflicted with. People who don't matter, that is, those who aren't in a position to please her in some way, would destroy her if she didn't proactively pound them into their place first. Her addictions include alcohol and crime shows.

Sandy Watkins is a social whore, or at least a puppy dog in search of a master, who derives his self-worth from the good opinions of others, a good opinion he tries hard to obtain. As a result, he has a strong need to take care of and be needed by others. He anticipates and takes the initiative to do research and assemble equipment. He readily sets aside his own interests and social activities in order to focus on those of Trice, Heller, and Samicki. He will continue "helping" Heller even when she becomes abusive and drives his ego even deeper underground. Work and the time machine project are the focus of his professional social interaction, and he becomes intensely unhappy with project problems. His behavior changes for each of the three, so that they won't reject him or become angry at him. Their disagreements and infighting scare and paralyze him emotionally. Naturally, he finds it difficult to say "no" even to conflicting demands. It is deeply upsetting if one of the three doesn't take his opinions and concerns seriously. He wants them to accept him and view him as essential, important, and special. That makes Watkins a first-class enabler and codependent.

Watkins' relationship with Heller is especially locked-in. She is happy to have a ready subject to validate her craving for power and control.

Vice President Bentler promises to take care of the needs of the populace in his speeches, but it's all just bait. He will tell people what they want to hear and promise them what they want in order to get their support, with no intention of following through. When his constituents express a need, it is an annoyance to him. None of his schemes are unthinkable or immoral; that only applies to the plans of others that block him from obtaining the power, prestige, and money that are rightfully his. Bentler is a charismatic narcissist, very tough, competitive, and domineering. He demands loyalty from subordinates but rarely returns the favor. He prefers to deal from a position of unquestioned power and overwhelming force, and makes no bones about it. He values toughness, believes that might makes right, and has utter contempt for the quality of mercy. Low-status and marginal groups provide him with an easy scapegoat to deflect everyone else's frustrations onto. He expects absolute obedience and believes he himself is infallible. Contrary facts and outcomes are either denied, spun, or projected and blamed on his enemies. Obstacles must be eliminated by every available means.

Roland Dauer will tell you what your first impression of him is. You will have no doubts at all about his genius and many accomplishments. He is in the habit of referring to himself in the third person, and is favorite word is "I," or rather "Dauer," and everything you say better be, and in fact, will be all about him. Every idea that comes to him, even or especially if it comes to him from a coworker's lips, will be first and immediately presented to his bosses so he is sure to get the credit for it, then he will tell everyone else. In response, genuflection is expected but not sufficient. He never tires of telling you about the minutiae of the problems he faces and solves every day, and you better not tire of it either, in fact failure to hang on his every word is an insult that proves your stupidity. Just realize that what he does is *very* important and you can't expect him to waste his valuable time and genius listening to *your* mundane issues. If you dare to suggest any ideas for improvement, he will twist it around and help you to understand that if there is any problem at all it is your fault. If there is merit to your suggestion, you can bet your next lunch he will get to his boss and present the idea as his own before you have take two steps in that direction yourself.

Vera Bleecker was probably not a totally conventional woman of her time, although what is known about her is piecemeal. The Bleeckers (or Bleekers; after a while various members of the family started dropping the 'c') were firmly rooted in Waterloo, Wisconsin until Harry O. Bleecker, the father, died in 1889 at age 29 after six years of marriage. He grew up in Wisconsin but his financial circumstances and occupation are unknown, although he might have been a farmer. After his death, his wife May I. Bleecker (maiden name Wright) was listed as having the occupation of "land owner." Harry had one surviving sister and four surviving brothers. His father, Vera's grandfather, George Bleecker (1820-1909), a businessman and farmer, was born in Canada in 1820 and immigrated to Waterloo where he came to own more than 800 acres of farm land, a lumber business, and a saw mill which he later sold. George was a self-made man who eschewed debt, one of fourteen children who was raised by an aunt and uncle. Perhaps his example of hard work, thrift, and ambition influenced his children and grandchildren as it certainly did son John R. (one of Vera's uncles).

No information could be found about his (George's) son Harry's (sometimes spelled Harrie in earlier references) personality or his relationship with his wife May and children Vera, Leslie, and Harrie Lyell. The Bleeckers remained in Waterloo until son Harrie (later references use "Harry" or "Lyell" as he preferred to be called) was away for his senior year of high school, then they moved to Appleton while Harrie Lyell and Vera obtained their degrees from Lawrence College.

In the absence of additional information, we can make several inferences about Vera Bleecker. She had one aunt only on her father's side of the family and was an only daughter (there were three aunts and an uncle on her mother's side of the family). As a result, we imagine she may have been a "daddy's girl." She therefore expected affection, approval, attention, and respect from men, and looked for someone like her childish image of her father, whatever that was. We assume that her father's untimely death left her with a fear of abandonment, resulted in her being careful about entering relationships, and meant that she looked for reciprocity from both family and friends. We might guess that the natural childish rivalry with her mother for her father's affection turned into a resented dependency, which resentment, however, would have become buried. It might have shown up in a disregard of her mother's approval or disapproval of some of her behavior. Would she have assigned any subconscious blame to her mother for her father's death? It is impossible to say.

The evidence clearly shows that she was supportive and caring toward brother Lyell and, by extension, others she felt close to. We further attribute normal, healthy 1900's values to her, supposing that she was giving, thoughtful, romantic, considerate, devoted, straightforward, thrifty, accepting, nurturing, and optimistic.

It is unknown what Vera did in Waterloo during the four years between her high school graduation and her freshman year at Lawrence. During 1900-1902 at least, neither of her brothers lived at home in Waterloo and were apparently away at school. Was Vera helping her mother and stifling her own ambitions while her brothers were at boarding school, and while brother Leslie was starting college? Probably so. Did her mother favor her brothers and that's why she didn't move to Appleton near Lawrence College until Lyell was almost ready to attend, or did she need help managing the family property in Waterloo? It's impossible to say.

While at Lawrence Vera participated in literary clubs, was active in the YWCA, helped produce the weekly school newspaper, and sang in choral groups. We glimpse Vera's personality through comments by classmates in the 1907-1908 "Ariel": she was described as always running, not having time for entertainment, and as having just one fault, a desire to control the Universe. An epitaph was ascribed to her, "She done noble." As a joke she was also the selfproclaimed secretary of the "Flunkers' Union."

In his freshman year, Lyell gave his reason for attending Lawrence as "I wanted a school where my sister could look after me. Last year she didn't seem to have much to do. It's good practice for her and makes things nice and easy for me." Lyell followed his sister's lead and jokingly designated himself a member of the "Sons of Rest," claiming to prefer that activity to all others. Thus, it appears that both of the Bleeckers had a healthy sense of humor, because under the surface they had to be hard working achievers like the rest of the Bleecker and Wright families of the time.

Romantic novels, "women's literature," were extremely popular in the early 1900s, and Vera Bleecker probably read her share. Possibly she participated in the prevalent belief in blissful romance and played the part: warm, supportive, caring, compassionate, and generous. On the other hand, she might have been totally careeroriented. We assume both here.

Vera's mother May and son Lyell moved again around 1911 after Lyell graduated. He became a teacher and a superintendent of schools and went on to graduate school as an education major at the University of Michigan. Son Leslie became a veterinary surgeon, like several other Wrights of the time.

Vera started a career as an English teacher after graduation in 1910, then moved up to a similar position in Oak Park (Chicago) soon thereafter. She also had a stated ambition to travel the world. Teaching was one of the few professions respected women could have at the time, in contrast to that of a reporter pursued by Edna Ferber, for example, although that limitation was lifting.

A controlling personality can be symptomatic of a number of things, such as a narcissistic user of people who views others as automatons to satisfy his or her wishes, or an obsessive-compulsive with emotional imperatives he or she *must* satisfy, or someone who desperately wants to avoid some source of pain or abuse they experienced earlier in their life, or a profoundly insecure individual, or some other source. As an only daughter whose father inexplicably died when she was four, it is perhaps likely Vera feared abandonment by anyone she became too close to and wanted to arrange things to prevent the compounded hurt that would result from a repeat occurrence. At least, that is the viewpoint assumed in this story.

Ian Larkin was noticeably introverted and smart. He didn't fit in very well and didn't care. His father determined he wanted Ian to attend school and have better opportunities than he had. He kept Ian from working the mines as a breaker boy except during school breaks. He also encouraged his son's interest in music, buying him a cheap mail-order piano. But the mine work Ian did do in the summer months when he was 10, 11, and 12 resulted in his being prone to asthma and respiratory difficulties. Despite his escape into reading, history, and music, his outlook was still noticeably parochial. He was influenced by some of the prejudice Edna Ferber complained about among some of the Welch miners in Ottumwa, Iowa, though he tried to be more broad-minded. Ferber complained that the miners' children in Ottumwa were idle, sullen, resentful loafers, but none of that described a normally busy Ian Larkin in Henderson, Kentucky. Ian and his father lived in a coal camp where the houses, merchandise store, church, and schools were owned by the coal company. He was not averse to an occasional drink or two with a friend, even to excess on rare occasions. As well, his language could sometimes be as rough as the place he grew up in. Ian tended to be even-tempered, inquisitive, and bookish with rough edges.

<u>Edna Ferber</u>, has been described as a crusader for "great causes"; gracious except when her wishes were disobeyed, in which case there was hell to pay; generous towards those she took a liking to; tough, engaged, charming, friendly, witty, unpredictable, having an enormous ego; and as tending to "play God." It is obvious Ferber was firmly in the extrovert camp. The best sources of information about her are her two autobiographies, the biography "Ferber" by her grandniece Julie Goldsmith Gilbert, and remembrances of those she encountered during her lifetime.

Certainly, there was anger and a sense of being special beneath a charming persona, an anger that could erupt unexpectedly, and which forced those around her to constantly "walk on eggshells." That describes the mature Edna Ferber, but this story has tried to be true to the character of the less mature 22-year-old version. Ferber apparently suppressed her anger most of the time as a young adult, taking it out as much on her older sister as on anyone else. Her sense of being more advanced than her contemporaries, which comes across in both of her autobiographies, may have resulted when she was thrust into a serious grown-up world right out of high school and acquitted herself quite admirably, even though she was unsure of herself at the beginning. In her autobiographies she shows in effect that young adults her age bored her with their trivial concerns. She came to believe, justifiably, that she was a very good reporter, learning quickly, and her young ambitions lain in that direction. Much of her anger may have stemmed from her treatment during seven childhood years in Ottumwa, Iowa, where she was often bullied for being Jewish. She did have many good experiences there too, however. There may also have been some resentment of her father, whose health was failing, and possibly some hidden anger that he couldn't fulfil his expected role, although she was a devoted and conscientious daughter.

The younger Ferber was not yet sure who she was; that didn't gel until her first successes as a fiction writer, although she was making clear strides in that direction. Even though Ferber had no desire to get married and have a family of her own, her extended family was important to her.

From childhood she was a natural storyteller who tended toward the romantic, even in some of her reporting at the Appleton Crescent (and particularly in her interviews). In addition, the Ferber family, particularly young Edna, were fond of the theater. In fact, Ferber's first ambition was to be an actress. These two traits no doubt served her well when she started writing fiction. Her noteworthy accomplishments included the novel "So Big" which won her a Pulitzer Prize, and her novel "Showboat," which Jerome Kern and Oscar Hammerstein II turned into a popular musical.

Ferber became an Appleton Crescent journalist in 1902 but was fired after 18 months by a new manager who didn't approve of women in the newsroom. She then went to work as a journalist for the Milwaukee Journal. In an age when women reporters wrote society, gossip and fashion columns, Ferber reported hard news, although he did also write a weekly (Saturday) society column at the Crescent.

Byron Beveridge saw himself as both a hard-nosed reporter and a patriot ready to do his duty as a member of the Wisconsin National Guard, where he steadily moved up in rank. He was comfortable in his local niche and not about to try and move up to a larger stage, that is, to a bigger newspaper or to the U.S. Army. Canadian born, he prided himself on being acquainted with a great many people in Appleton and on his network of local news sources. Edna Ferber described him as "a lanky cadaverous chap who had been a lieutenant in the Spanish-American war and was a great Company G boy and man-about town. He wasn't warm or even an engaging personality, but he knows everyone, everyone knew him, his lank stoop-shouldered figure ranged around town in a lope."

The Saecker Brothers, all of whom were born in Germany, were prominent businessmen in Appleton from the 1880s. Politically, the Saecker brothers were staunch Republicans and apparently active in local politics; W. F. Saecker served two terms on the Appleton city council and was the first president of the Outaganie County Board of Libraries starting in 1901. The families were active in the Appleton Methodist Episcopal Church.

Wilhelm Frederich Saecker (W. F. or "William", the oldest born in 1852) was president and part owner of the Appleton Machine Company, which initially had seven men on its payroll but grew rapidly until it employed around sixty. Blacksmithing was part of his background as a teenager. The company specialized in custom contract and repair work and later in papermaking machinery. He also had an interest in the Union Toy and Furniture Company, which grew to 40 employees and where he was treasurer and manager, and he was a part owner of the Saecker Brothers' funeral business. He was also a first vice president of the Wisconsin Funeral Directors Association, a Mason, and a member of the Temple of Honor (a secret fraternal order similar to the Masons and the Odd Fellows which promoted temperance).

Franz Edward Saecker (F. E. or "Frank," born in 1854) was secretary and part owner of the Appleton Machine Company. He was president of the furniture business and part owner of the funeral business.

Hermann Gustav Saecker (H. G., the youngest of the three surviving brothers, born in 1858) was secretary-treasurer of the Appleton Machine Company and had an interest in the funeral and furniture businesses. He served as a fire and police commissioner.

Ada Saecker Pfitzner-Saverni was a daughter of W. F. Saecker. She graduated from Lawrence in 1902, furthered her studies in Europe and New York, married a German Kapellmeister, and went on to have a notable career as an opera singer in Europe, Canada, and the U.S.

Appleton, Wisconsin: At the turn of the twentieth century, most small towns had their own unique character, personality, and history. Local events dominated. It wasn't like today where you find the same national chain stores and restaurants along with similar strip malls and tract houses wherever you go, and where everyone in the country gets their news, entertainment and much of their outlook from the same mass media. Towns were more unique in their character than they are today and were as varied as people. The city of Appleton in 1900 struck the author as particularly interesting among those he has read about. It had its share of notable citizens. It was not at all isolated, because large cities such as Chicago and Milwaukee were easily accessible to its residents. It is as much a character in the story as the people who lived there.

Note on street addresses: The street numbering for Appleton changed in 1924 and a few streets were apparently renamed over the years as well. This story is based on the historical names and uses the street number and topological features present in 1907. These will not correspond to modern maps or mapping software.

Addendum Two
Elements of the Story

<u>Time Travel and Cause-and-Effect</u>

History is an extremely complex system, with many elements interacting in many possible ways.

Complex systems tend strongly towards unpredictability. Cause and effect might be entirely disproportionate. In other words, a slight change can sometimes dramatically alter the future course of events while, on the other hand, the system may adapt or evolve so that a major event causes only minor, even unnoticeable changes.

Famous examples include the butterfly effect (Edward Norton Lorenz, chaos theory), where a butterfly flaps its wings in Brazil starting an unforeseeable chain reaction that results in a thunderstorm in New York City, and the sandpile simulation (Bak–Tang–Wiesenfeld model), where grains are dropped on the pile one at a time with varying effects until one single grain happens to land on just the right spot that causes the entire pile to collapse.

On the other hand, comets and asteroids whiz about the hinterlands of countless stars, pulling on each other, colliding, breaking apart, feeling the merest nudge from a distant passing star, changing orbits ever so slightly, all with absolutely no consequence beyond the individual icy rocks themselves. The universe quickly forgets and no notice is ever taken. That is, except for the once in a trillion times when a mere millimeter displacement in an asteroid a billion miles away sends it in on a path that one day, millennia later, crashes into a planet.

Molecules evolve changing atom by atom. Once in a hundred thousand sequences the cumulative change becomes significant, evolution, producing chlorophyll or insulin. But change the order of two atomic alterations and a different molecule results. Then there is no backtracking to take a different fork in the road and, for example, there is no chlorophyll or insulin, and life hits a dead end. The opportunity to produce these molecules is likely lost forever. Some other molecule and biological process takes their place.

There is the chance late arrival, though only by seconds, that means missing a rare but significant event. There is the reliably repeating pattern that unexpectedly falls short. There is that one time in a billion when the timing is wrong with shattering consequences.

This, then, is the fire the time traveler plays with. He has a power that is amplified far beyond the reach of the craziest megalomaniac. Eryk Samicki sticks his toe into the edge of that sea and withdraws it, but not without consequence. Has he learned anything? Did he gain any wisdom? Now that the time machine is proven, inexorable forces were releases, the imperatives of the human shadow-mind, to ensure that the machine will be used by someone. Does Eryk know enough to safely navigate the future time travels he must undertake? And who will control the machine?

The benevolent time traveler might think he can be the unobtrusive observer, recording and not affecting. But how can he possibly be? People are programmed to react to their surroundings, to react to others. He has to eat and sleep somewhere, to stay alive, to satisfy his basic needs. Even his mere passive presence is bound to be noticed. Is anything about him strange or out of place? No, the observer with his butterfly wings must still interact, he can't help it.

It gets worse. There is a hypothesis, and equations to support it, that the indeterminacies of quantum mechanics are not inherent in matter and energy but result from interacting countless parallel universes. Does the time traveler then disrupt the cause and effect of countless other universes when he goes back and makes a change? Is his havoc then on an unimaginable multi-universe scale?

It's all much too complex to comprehend. We can only follow the story, cross our fingers, and hope no malevolent creature gets their hands on the time machine, so we don't then suddenly vanish without a trace or a sound or any record we were ever here.

<u>Moral Dilemma</u>

What if you are in a situation where all of your choices are morally wrong? What if it's a devil's choice? How do you decide what to do?

What if yours is a Hobson's choice (having to choose which is the least undesirable thing; the story is about an innkeeper named Hobson who rented horses to students).

Eryk's choice is whether to lie about himself or tell the truth and consequently, either change history, possibly condemning living people to the death of having never been born, or being committed as a nut case and maybe never returning as a result, again altering history. His only moral choice is to return at once to his own time to avoid any chance of interaction. However, he has no control over that because communication between past and present is not possible.

He could have avoided the dilemma in the first place by never time traveling at all, but then someone else would certainly have gone instead, maybe someone like Heller, whose motives are less than pure. Eryk must assume his own time travel is the least of the evils and he should therefore go himself.

The other option is for Eryk to travel back in time, try to minimize the changes he brings about, then find a way to repair the damage upon his return.

All of this is overly simplistic.

First of all, how do you know what's the best thing to do? Morals and values depend on culture, country, family, individual experience, and many other factors. There are the values of Puritan New England, Southern values, Plains Indian values, the values of a lawless 19th century Western boom town, the values of a fanatic or of fanatic cultures or cults such as that of a Jonesville, small town 19th century values versus current big city values, and on and on. Not to mention that morals and values can be situational. Are there no absolutes? In 1907, the English-speaking world had passed from the Victorian era to the Gilded Age to the Progressive Era, each age leaving its residual mark contributing to the progressive culture. Should Eryk do the right thing based on 1907 Progressive Era morals, on modern ideas, or on his personal principles?

And what if the time traveler witnesses a flagrant wrong, say a brutal assault, an attempted murder, or a lynching? What is his moral obligation? Should he intervene and prevent the crime, saving a life that will then go on to add offspring or something else to human history and thus change it, or is he morally bound to turn his back?

Since the time traveler must exchange himself with some other complex living thing, what does he do with the life he now represents? Should he perpetuate the mistakes of that life, however misguided, misinformed, tragic, unenlightened, or conversely uplifting, or is he morally bound to improve upon it? Should he feel free to indulge in whatever vices that life embraced?

Are there any absolute standards in the first place? Maybe. Basic human social instincts presuppose concepts such as fairness, ownership, social justice, cooperation and competition, social reciprocity, distaste for cognitive dissonance, and numerous others. These are built in to the human psyche and are interpreted and scripted based on culture and nurture. They exist and are grounded in the context of the laws by which the universe operates. Maybe, therefore, there are absolute moral standards on a per-species basis. Getting to the root of this problem and subjecting it to rigorous analysis is no easy matter.

This might be a subject for a Ph.D. dissertation. The author apologizes for not having one available.

Eryk was probably not thinking about any of this. Like everyone else, he would have been driven by the unexamined assumptions and assertions of twenty-first century America, by his own unique and therefore idiosyncratic experience, by unreachable subconscious drives, and by the scantly examined and disowned shadow and compensatory forces of his own unconscious. Even Trice, the rigidly self-controlled obsessive-compulsive order freak, is having an affair (or trying to anyway), something that violates his own rules of order and authority. Yet he doesn't see the contradiction. The struggle is hidden from his own self.

<u>Playing God</u>

Going back in history can mean playing God, accidently or on purpose, unless the time traveler can somehow discipline himself or herself to be a completely uninvolved fly on the wall. Even if the traveler has no intention of interfering, time travel puts him or her in a powerful position. As William Pit the Elder said, "Unlimited power is apt to corrupt the minds of those who possess it"

<u>Would it be Obvious That Eryk is Out of Place?</u>

Things will change and there's no stopping it. Since 1907, manner of speech, accents, slang, word meanings, science and medicine, cultural beliefs and assumptions, social and behavior standards, education levels, levels of individual sophistication, and popular superstitions and biases all are different.

Misunderstandings and faux pas based on changed word meanings, and inadvertent use of inappropriate recent expressions are possible. As examples, Eryk isn't likely to allow a doctor to bleed him out or give him some alcohol-laden elixir as a cure for an infectious disease. He had better not let the acronyms DNA, WTF, OMG or LOL creep into his speech, and he had better pretend to be properly shocked over the things lingering Victorian standards deemed obscene. Words change their meanings over time, for example, "punk" originally meant a prostitute, then in the early 1900s it came to mean a criminal's assistant, whereas today it means a disreputable and inexperienced person; in 1900 "livid" was a blue-grey color and nothing more.

Eryk is aware of history, technology, scientific discoveries, and social changes after 1907. His knowledge of these things can't be erased and it would be difficult for him not to act on it or make accidental references to it. There are myriad ways Eryk could betray himself. Could his preparation overcome the many tell-tale signs? A trained eye like that of a seasoned reporter would probably notice straightaway that something was off. What about the average person?

<u>Other Eras</u>

Clearly, each age has its own unique feeling and circumstances. Each has its own counter-reaction and its own countercurrents under the surface that lead to a new and different age. Within each age, each country has its own unique characteristics, and within that each town, and within that each social group, and within that each family, and within that each individual, and within each individual his or her competing drives and ambitions, like a fractal pattern that keeps recurring on a finer and finer scale until you get down to the individual atoms of the human psyche and the environment.

The progressive era was a period of great optimism and hope. Like the Renaissance, minds and actions felt freed and liberated from rules and restrictions that had restrained them in the past. People felt good about themselves and their future. People believed in progress and did not question that every generation would have a better life than the one before. There were naysayers, pessimists, and victims as always. There was also plenty of poverty during this period, especially among new immigrants, but there was also the expectation that with hard work and dedication anyone could rise above it (a third of all immigrants returned to their native countries, demonstrating that it was still a struggle). Progressives believed that exploitation, discrimination, disenfranchisement, and other evils of the day as they defined them could be overcome in time by group action.

Contrast this with periods and places where people lived with shortages of basic necessities and struggled under the oppressive, stifling, heavy hand of dictatorships such as those of Stalin and Ceausescu. They are all very different eras indeed.

World War I forced many changes. The mortal danger and seriousness of the war gave way to a counter-reaction, the roaring twenties, which was part of a transition period to the next era. Like an artistic, literary, or musical talent manifest in one generation which then disappears entirely in the next, only to reappear again in the following generation, the financial debauchery necessary to pay for the war became established, and it progressed until it was one of the precipitating factors in the Great Depression, the next era that was entirely different from what came before and that left its scars on the generations that followed. World War II, the late forties and fifties, the sixties counter-culture drop-out groups, and other eras that followed each had their own distinct feel, their own values and life-styles.

The current era is again one of great scientific progress, but the nearly universal optimism and faith in institutions and in the future that were omnipresent in the Progressive era are no longer there.

People may become creatures of their formative years and then no longer fit in when the culture transforms into its next form. They become old-fashioned throw-backs and fuddy-duddies unless they adapt.

How would it be, then, if you were transported to a different era? Could you fit in? Would you be able to alter your outlook and beliefs and align them with the period, or would you stick to your habits and have other people think you were strange?